MYSTERY AT MEAD'S MOUNTAIN

Trixie
Belden

Your TRIXIE BELDEN Library

1 The Secret of the Mansion
2 The Red Trailer Mystery
3 The Gatehouse Mystery
4 The Mysterious Visitor
5 The Mystery Off Glen Road
6 Mystery in Arizona
7 The Mysterious Code
8 The Black Jacket Mystery
9 The Happy Valley Mystery
10 The Marshland Mystery
11 The Mystery at Bob-White Cave
12 The Mystery of the Blinking eye
13 The Mystery on Cobbett's Island
14 The Mystery of the Emeralds
15 Mystery on the Mississippi
16 The Mystery of the Missing Heiress
17 The Mystery of the Uninvited Guest
18 The Mystery of the Phantom Grasshopper
19 The Secret of the Unseen Treasure
20 The Mystery Off Old Telegraph Road *(new)*
21 The Mystery of the Castaway Children *(new)*
22 Mystery at Mead's Mountain *(new)*

Trixie Belden and MYSTERY AT MEAD'S MOUNTAIN

BY KATHRYN KENNY

Cover by Jack Wacker

® GOLDEN PRESS
Western Publishing Company, Inc.
Racine, Wisconsin

0-307-21593-8

CONTENTS

MYSTERY AT MEAD'S MOUNTAIN

Mr. Wheeler's Plan • 1

TRIXIE, TRIXIE, wait up!" called Honey, pushing her way through the crowded corridor of Sleepyside-on-the-Hudson Junior-Senior High School.

"Honey Wheeler, where have you been?" demanded Trixie. She tossed her short blond curls in pretended anger, but the twinkle in her blue eyes showed that she wasn't really upset with her best friend. "I waited outside your math class so we could go to lunch together. When you didn't come out, I decided you'd already gone to your locker, but you weren't there either. Come on, I'm famished!"

"I got called out of math to take a phone call," Honey explained as the two girls joined the flow of hall traffic. "It was Daddy calling from his office in

New York. He asked me to invite all of the Bob-Whites to a special dinner tonight. He said you should all come early and exercise the horses before dinner. And listen to this," she commanded, her normally calm voice full of excitement. "After dinner he wants to discuss something with us. He won't tell me what it is. All he said was it's a surprise he thinks we'll really like!"

"Gleeps!" Trixie exclaimed. "Your father comes up with the neatest surprises, like the trips to Cobbett's Island and St. Louis, and the Bob-White station wagon, not that we can afford to keep it, with the cost of insurance and all. Do you think it's something really neat like that?"

"I don't have any idea, Trixie. You and your brothers will come, won't you?" Honey begged.

"Of course—" Trixie began. Then she moaned. They had been walking down the stairs, and abruptly Trixie sat down on a step. "Today is the day before the garden club's Christmas bazaar," she said gloomily. "Moms is in charge of it, and Brian, Mart, and I promised to go over there right after school and help her set up booths. We'll probably be there till late tonight. I'd much rather go riding and hear what your father has to say than set up—yipes!" She jumped to her feet to avoid being trampled by a crowd of boys that came thundering down the stairs.

Honey took Trixie's arm and pulled her out of the way. "You and your brothers have got to come," she pleaded. "Why don't you call your mother just to see what she says? Maybe the three of you could come over for dessert," she suggested.

"Good idea," agreed Trixie, her face brightening. "I just know your father's got something really exciting to discuss, and Moms can be pretty softhearted around Christmastime. Maybe if we promise to work super hard until time for dessert. . . ."

"Your mother is softhearted all the time, Trixie Belden, and you know it. I'd come and help with the bazaar if I could, but Regan will have a fit if *some*one isn't there to exercise the horses."

"We certainly don't need Regan upset with us," Trixie decided. "If he quit, then your father would be mad at us because he could never find another groom like Regan. He'd probably be so mad he'd forget to tell us his surprise!"

Honey laughed. "Go call your mother," she said, giving Trixie a gentle shove. "I'll meet you at our table. I want to tell the other Bob-Whites about the surprise."

As Trixie made her way down the hall toward the pay phone, she thought of how much Honey's friendship meant to her. So much had happened since they'd met each other. Probably the most important thing was the forming of the Bob-Whites of the Glen, the club that included Trixie, her look-alike brother, Mart, and their older brother, Brian. Honey and her adopted brother, Jim Frayne, were also members, along with Diana Lynch, who was fourteen like Trixie and Honey, and Dan Mangan, nephew of Regan, the Wheelers' groom.

Knowing Honey had also led to all of the mysteries.

Shortly after Trixie and Honey became friends, things just started "happening," and the two found themselves constantly involved in solving mysteries. Handsome Jim Frayne had been the subject of two of their first cases. Their mysteries kept life very exciting for all of the Bob-Whites.

Friendship with Honey had meant many grand times at Manor House, the Wheeler estate. It was a large mansion with extensive grounds that included stables, a lake, and a three-hundred-acre game preserve.

Trixie thought affectionately of her own mother, who worked so hard making a nice home for her family at Crabapple Farm, and of her father, who worked at the bank in Sleepyside. Trixie found satisfaction in working for what she had, and she appreciated the Bob-Whites' policy of each member's contributing to the club only money that he or she had earned.

She felt so lucky to have the nicest family and the best friends in the entire world. And on top of all that, there was always another mystery waiting to be solved. Maybe Mr. Wheeler's surprise would lead to still another . . . *if* she could just get Moms to let them go for dessert.

By the time Trixie joined the Bob-Whites at their usual table in the cafeteria, they had almost finished eating and were busy speculating about Mr. Wheeler's surprise.

"Pray tell, lunchless lady, what tidings thou bearest," hailed Mart, who loved to use fancy language to tease his sister. "Not that you'll be lunchless for long," he added dryly.

"If you mean 'what's the news,' I can tell you the news is good," retorted Trixie between bites of her tuna fish sandwich. "Moms says okay for dessert—and for dinner, too!"

Amid the Belden boys' cheers, Trixie continued, "Moms got more done today than she thought she would, so we just have to help with some last-minute things. We'll have to help right up until dinner, though. So the ride is out. Moms didn't have any idea what Mr. Wheeler's surprise is. Do you, Jim?"

"Not even a notion, but the only way to find out is to wait and see," he said philosophically, looking at Honey's apple wistfully. "Sisters sure come in handy, don't they?" he observed after Honey motioned that she'd had enough to eat.

"Hmmm," Trixie mused, lost in thought, "this is all very mysterious, isn't it?"

"Nothing's mysterious about having a handy sister, just lucky," gibed Mart, eyeing Trixie's apple. "I myself am not that lucky, cursed as I am with an ever-ravenous kinswoman."

Trixie took a deliberately noisy bite out of her apple. "I don't mean about sisters, birdbrain," she said, "I mean about Mr. Wheeler's surprise."

"Maybe we'd better quit thinking about that for now and get down to something more urgent—our Bob-White car," Brian said. "In case you've all forgotten, the first of the year is coming up, which means our car insurance payment is due."

"Ouch," remarked Mart, who was the treasurer of the club. "Our coffers are unlikely to withstand the strain of buying a postage stamp to mail the payment, much less buying the insurance itself!"

"We'll just have to earn some money," Trixie said. "Christmas vacation is coming up. We'll have to find work."

"If you keep eating like that," teased Mart, "you'll make a fine department-store Santa Claus, minus the beard."

"Cut it out, Mart," said Trixie. "There's got to be lots of odd jobs we could do."

"Nothing that would bring in as much money as we need," Mart argued. "Let's be realistic. . . ."

"Knock it off, you two," Jim broke in. "But Mart's right, Trixie. It would take a long time to earn as much as we need doing odd jobs."

The bell rang, signaling the end of the lunch period.

"Things will work out," Trixie insisted, finishing up her apple. "They always do when we set our minds to it."

"Personally, I don't think there's anything we can do but sell the car," said Brian seriously.

"We can't let that happen!" cried Di.

"Maybe Daddy will give us the money," Honey suggested. "We just can't lose the Bob-White car!"

"Honey, you know the club rule about contributing only money we earn ourselves," Jim reminded her.

"One thing is sure," Dan put in. "If we sold the car, we'd have enough for the insurance."

"I think we're too upset to think straight," Jim decided. "Why don't we just let it simmer in the back of our minds till tonight? After Dad finishes talking with us, we can have a special Bob-White meeting to sort everything out."

The others agreed that was a good idea and then hurried off to their classes.

All during dinner that evening, Mr. Wheeler kept from mentioning his surprise and teasingly changed the subject whenever someone else mentioned it. Finally, after a delicious dessert of French pastries, the Bob-Whites, Mr. and Mrs. Wheeler, and Miss Trask, the manager of the Wheeler household, all settled into comfortable chairs in the living room.

"Mmmm," Mart groaned, patting his stomach, "that roast venison from your game preserve was the *pièce de résistance* of an outstanding meal. I couldn't eat another bite, and that's really saying something."

"We love to have you here, Mart," said Mrs. Wheeler pleasantly. "Cook is especially delighted—you appreciate her efforts so much."

"I can't think of a nobler goal in life than delighting Cook," said Mart grandly. "Anyone who has elevated cuisine to such an art deserves as much delight as possible. Matter of fact . . ."

"Jeepers, Mart, let Mr. Wheeler talk! Please, won't you tell us your surprise now, Mr. Wheeler?" begged Trixie.

Mr. Wheeler laughed indulgently at Trixie's impatience but agreed that it was time to break the suspense. He got up and strode across the room to the fireplace. He leaned against it, his bright red hair contrasting vividly with the snowy woods scene in the priceless painting that hung over the mantel.

"As you all know," he began, "my company is involved in many business ventures, and we're always looking for promising new investments. Do you remember George Kimball, our neighbor at Cobbett's Island?"

"Sure," Jim answered. "We had a great time swimming and sailing with his son, Peter."

"Do you remember that George was looking for a ski lodge to buy?" prompted Mr. Wheeler.

"Oh, yes," recalled Honey. "Did he find one?"

"He found the beginnings of one and approached me with a very special plan for it," her father replied. "He and I may become partners in the venture. It's in a beautiful area of Vermont. Originally there was going to be a fancy resort and a full-scale downhill ski course. However, the developers have had a number of problems and are ready to give up. Before running out of patience and financing, they managed to build a very nice lodge, several rope tows, and one chair lift. What George and I hope to do is turn the entire project into a *natural* recreation area, leaving the land as undisturbed as possible. In the winter, there'd be cross-country skiing, snowshoeing, and skating, with camping, fishing, and hiking in the summer. We'd keep the social center and restaurant at the lodge open year-round."

"Dad, that's terrific!" exclaimed Jim.

"We really need more natural recreation areas in

this country," Brian agreed.

"I'm glad you feel that way," beamed Mr. Wheeler, "because we're hoping to aim this project at spirited young people like you. George and I have decided we've got to get firsthand impressions from that type of person. I am hiring a group of professionals to study all the facilities and make a full report back to me, but they won't be able to give me that young person's viewpoint."

Trixie sucked in her breath. She suddenly knew what Mr. Wheeler was going to say next.

"So I also want to send in others who *can* give me that information," continued Mr. Wheeler, his voice businesslike but his eyes twinkling. "And I don't know anyone who would do a better job than the Bob-Whites. That is, if you want the job. . . ."

Mr. Wheeler found himself drowned out by a chorus of shouts: "Wow!" "Terrific!" "You're kidding!" "Gleeps!" "What does he mean, do we want the job?!"

Then level-headed Brian spoke up. "But, sir, I really don't see how we could possibly take the job, what with school and our chores and all."

Mr. Wheeler walked back to his chair and sat down. "That's why I wanted to get you all here tonight," he said, unperturbed. "We want to get started right away. With the Christmas holidays coming up next week, I thought you might like to go then."

"It sounds fantastic, Mr. Wheeler, but we Beldens can't possibly go," said Trixie despondently. "Moms and Dad are planning a big open house on Saturday, the twenty-sixth. They'll need all of our help."

"For shame, Trixie," Mr. Wheeler chuckled. "I wouldn't think of letting you and the boys leave until you help your parents with the vast mountain of dirty dishes they're going to have. And speaking of mountain," he went on, noting the hopeful expression returning to Trixie's face, "that's the name of the lodge—Mead's Mountain. The plan would be for all of you and Miss Trask to fly up to Groverville—which is about half an hour from Mead's Mountain—on my private plane Saturday night, after everything is cleaned up from your party. If you stay for a week, that should be enough time to get the feel of the place, and you will have a day or two to rest up at home before going back to school again. I'd go with you, but Mrs. Wheeler and I will be leaving that morning for business in Alaska."

"This would all sound terrific if we could get Moms and Dad to agree," said Brian excitedly. "Do you think we can, Mart?"

"Don't ask me," said Mart, his eyes closing. "I'm already whizzing across the countryside in the gelid mountain air, stimulating my appetite for a nourishing cup of hot chocolate sipped before a roaring fire. . . ."

"Oh, I have a feeling your parents will agree," Miss Trask answered Brian confidently. "Why don't we tell them the history of Mead's Mountain?" she suggested, turning to Mr. Wheeler. "I'm sure they'd be interested, especially Trixie."

"Uh-oh." Mart snapped to attention. "You did say *Mead's* Mountain, not *Mystery* Mountain, correct?"

Mr. Wheeler grinned. "Yes, the mountain is named

after Thomas L. Mead, one of the first trappers in that area. He was a cranky character who wasn't very friendly. When other people started to settle in that territory, he tried to drive them out by burning their cabins and crops. In spite of his efforts, the town of Groverville was established. Eventually he was caught and hanged in the town square. From that time on, whenever something unexplained would occur, the townspeople would blame it on the ghost of Thomas Mead, later known as the ghost of Mead's Mountain. In fact, some people even claimed to have seen a ghostly man with long white hair wandering around the mountain."

Despite Mart's sarcastic query, Trixie felt a small shiver of excitement and fear go down her spine.

"For example," Mr. Wheeler continued, "when problems cropped up with the plans to build the downhill ski resort on the mountain, some people said the lodge must be haunted."

"What type of things went wrong, Mr. Wheeler?" asked Dan.

"Oh, normal things that can plague any large business venture," he replied. "They had trouble getting enough financing, and trouble with the unions, and on top of that, some equipment breakdowns. But the resort is finally operating on a limited scale now. A young couple, Pat and Katie O'Brien, are the new caretakers. I told them I'd let them know tomorrow if you're coming. I hope you can all let me know tonight. Of course, all your expenses will be paid, and then there's the matter of salary. . . ."

"Oh, you don't have to pay us!" cried Trixie. "Why, this is really a super vacation for us!"

"Trixie's absolutely right," Brian agreed. "You've always done so much for the Bob-Whites, sir. We'd love the opportunity to repay you a little."

Honey's mother smiled. "You knew they'd feel that way, didn't you, Matthew?"

"Yes, I did," said Mr. Wheeler, "but I also know that that team of professionals simply won't be able to give me the young person's opinion I need."

"You really *need* us?" Di asked, her violet eyes widening with disbelief.

"I certainly do," Mr. Wheeler insisted. "But I've thought of an alternative proposal to paying you a salary. Honey and Jim have told me you've been thinking of selling the Bob-Whites' car because of the high insurance payment. I would be happy to make this year's payment for you if you'll only do this favor for me."

"Mr. Wheeler, you're sensational!" squealed Di.

"I just knew things would work out!" Trixie said triumphantly.

"But, Dad," Jim said hesitantly, "you know we hate to take money unless we earn it."

"You'll earn it—don't worry about that," said Mr. Wheeler heartily. "Wait till you see my lists of questions and points to look for. And I expect a detailed, typed report within the week after you get back. So, is it a deal, pending parental approval, of course?" he asked, his eyes twinkling mischievously.

"It's a deal!" chorused the Bob-Whites.

"Come on, let's go see what our folks say," urged Trixie.

Then Dan, who had been unusually silent for a while, spoke up. "I can give you my answer now," he said sadly. "I'm afraid I can't go. I promised Judge Harding I'd spend the vacation working with the young kids from the juvenile home."

Someday Dan hoped to be a policeman so he could work full time with kids in trouble. He spent as much time as he could, between studying and helping out on the game preserve, working with children and their problems. He had come a long way since the days when he had been a scared, hostile problem himself.

"Oh, Dan, it won't be nearly as much fun without you," complained Di.

"And you skate so well—you'd probably have a ball on skis," Jim said.

"I'm sure those little kids will be happy to have you, though," added Honey.

"I'm sorry you can't make it, Dan," said Mr. Wheeler. "We'll have to make sure you get up there sometime next year. Will the rest of you let me know as soon as possible, please?"

It wasn't long before Trixie was able to phone Honey with the news that the Beldens had permission to go.

"Do you know that your sneaky father called Moms this morning and told her his whole plan?" Trixie asked. "She and my dad knew all along and didn't say anything!"

"You're kidding!" Honey exclaimed. "Who would have guessed our parents could keep secrets so well?"

"It's a good thing your dad didn't let Bobby in on the secret," Trixie commented, "or it would have been let out of the bag ages ago."

"Oh, Trixie, I'm so excited I can hardly sit still," Honey rushed on. "Di just called to say she can come. Imagine—a whole week in the mountains!"

"Gleeps, Honey, *I'm* so excited I don't know how I'm going to get through the next week! Are we going to need any special clothes or equipment?"

"Daddy says we will probably spend most of the time cross-country skiing," Honey replied. "He's going to go over all the details with Jim and me tonight so we can fill the rest of you in tomorrow."

"Cross-country skiing? I've never done that before. Neither have Brian and Mart," said Trixie in a dubious tone.

"Jim and I haven't either, but Daddy says we'll catch on in no time," Honey assured her. "We'll be able to rent skis there, but we'll have to bring our own ski clothes. Long underwear, ski pants, sweaters, and a windbreaker—you know, lightweight stuff. Oh, and Daddy says to bring a swimsuit, too, because there's a pool at the lodge."

"Wow! Say, Honey, do you think we'll need a dress?" Trixie asked hesitantly. She really hated to get dressed up.

"Gee, I don't think so," Honey replied, glad to set her friend at ease. "You could throw in some extra jeans to wear around the lodge."

"Whew!" said Trixie. "I've got to go now. Bobby's ready for bed, and I have to read him to sleep. Lucky for me, he's really tired from helping Moms with the bazaar this afternoon."

"He is such a doll," Honey said. "You're lucky to have a little brother, Trixie."

"I know he can be awfully cute at times, but other times he can be a real pest! I'll see you on the bus tomorrow."

As Trixie hung up the phone, a slow smile crossed her lips. She hadn't mentioned it to anyone yet, but she had a hunch that the so-called ghost of Mead's Mountain held the promise of a new mystery waiting for her.

Swirls in the Snow • 2

THE DAYS BEFORE CHRISTMAS flew by. Almost before Trixie knew it, she and the rest of her family were cleaning up after the Belden open house the day after Christmas. The party had been fun, but Trixie had been afraid that clean-up time, and thus departure time, would never arrive. Besides, she couldn't wait to change out of the party dress she found so uncomfortable and into jeans and a sweater.

Finally, she was free to go finish her packing. She was just asking Brian to help her get her suitcase shut, when they heard the doorbell ring. It was Tom Delanoy, the Wheelers' chauffeur, who had the rest of the Bob-Whites and Miss Trask outside in the car and was taking them all to the airport.

Trixie, Brian, and Mart bounded downstairs to the front door, where they exchanged farewell hugs with their parents and Bobby. The youngest Belden was unhappy with his siblings for "deserting" him during Christmas vacation.

"But think how much fun you'll have with your presents," Trixie said, giving Bobby an extra squeeze. "Especially your books. Maybe by the time we get back, you'll be able to read yourself to sleep!"

Bobby brightened a bit, and Mrs. Belden laughed. "Dan said he'd stop over to visit Bobby," she said. "But that's no excuse for you three not to hurry back soon. Have a safe trip!"

Waving and laughing, the Belden trio went outside and squeezed into the already crowded car. "Would anyone like to see my imitation of a sardine?" Mart asked rhetorically.

When Tom pulled the car up to the airport, Bob Murphy, Mr. Wheeler's congenial pilot, came out to greet them. "I'm glad to see the famous Bob-Whites again," he said, winking at Miss Trask.

"I'm going along with them to make sure they don't become notorious, Bob," bantered Miss Trask, who looked as trim as ever in her sturdy winter coat and sensible boots.

Bob asked them to sign in on the plane's log, and Trixie dutifully filled in her name and address. "What shall I write under 'purpose of trip'?" she wondered.

"Investigative team to analyze ski resort in order to facilitate business negotiations," Mart suggested.

"Don't be silly, Mart," Trixie giggled. "I could never

spell all those ridiculous words."

"I knew we should have given you a dictionary for Christmas instead of ski pants," he muttered.

"You probably can't spell it any better than I can," Trixie retorted hotly. "Brian, will you fill this in?"

Brian took the pencil and said, "Mart, I'll guarantee our sister will get far more use out of the ski pants than she would from a dictionary. Hey, next it asks for 'name of company.' "

"The Belden-Wheeler Detective Agency," Trixie told him pertly.

Jim and Mart hooted. "Better make that 'Schoolgirl Shamuses and Company,' " Mart scoffed.

"I'll just write in 'Bob-White Investigators,' " said Brian diplomatically.

When they all crowded into the small airplane, Trixie asked Bob if she could sit next to him for a while. She was curious to see what the pilot's view would be during takeoff, especially at night.

Bob seemed to appreciate her interest and waved her toward the large, comfortable seat next to him in the cockpit. In front of their seats were the small control wheel and instrument panel. There were so many dials and gauges on the panel that it almost made Trixie dizzy to look at it.

Over the radio came a voice from the control tower, giving them clearance for takeoff. As the little plane surged down the runway, gaining speed with every foot, Trixie felt as though the plane were melting away and she were flying all by herself. Then she realized that it was the ground that was melting away.

They were airborne without her being aware that they had even left the ground.

Trixie listened to the roaring of the engines in front of her and the hum of the Bob-Whites' voices behind her. Except for the blue runway lights reflecting a path in the white snow, the entire world was black. Slowly the blue lights, too, faded from sight, and the blackness completely enfolded Trixie.

Jeepers, she thought. *It's so peaceful and lovely up here. There's a kind of warmth and safeness about everything being so completely dark.*

Bob broke into her thoughts. "We're about leveled off, Trixie. Would you like to fly for a while?"

"What? Me fly? Really? But I don't know how!" Trixie fluttered.

"At this point, there's nothing to it," Bob said reassuringly. "You just hold the control wheel and keep the plane going straight ahead. You pull back to ascend and push forward to descend. Turn the wheel to the left for a left bank, to the right for a right bank. It's a lot like driving a car, except there's no reverse and the streets aren't as crowded."

"I can't drive a car either," Trixie told the pilot truthfully.

"No problem," insisted Bob. "Flying a plane can be easier. We have to stay at this level and on this course, unless we get permission to change or there's an emergency. That's required by safety regulations and sky courtesy."

Under Bob's guidance, Trixie tried each of the basic maneuvers. Abruptly he said, "Just keep it on course,

Trixie. I'm going to get a cup of coffee from Miss Trask."

Trixie forced a laugh. "You're joking."

"Nope—you're doing great! Don't worry, though, I'm not going to leave my seat. Do you want anything?"

Trixie shook her head, and Bob turned around in his seat to talk to Miss Trask. Then it dawned on Trixie that she *was* flying all by herself. She alone was steering the plane into the endless stretch of darkness ahead.

Maybe I should add learning to fly to my list of things I'm going to do someday, she thought.

Then, with no warning, the plane started to drop out of the sky!

Trixie stifled a scream. *Now, don't panic,* she told herself as she slowly pulled back on the controls.

Nothing happened.

Okay, now *you can panic,* she decided, opening her mouth to yell for Bob and pulling harder on the controls.

But Bob was already taking over the control wheel. Again without warning, the plane leveled off and seemed to bounce back up into the sky.

"Whew!" Trixie breathed as she sank back into her seat. She was pale and shaking. "I thought we were goners! You can't imagine what an awful feeling that is."

"You did fine, Trixie," Bob said cheerfully. "That was terrific the way you didn't panic."

Trixie blushed to the roots of her hair. "I was panicking plenty," she protested.

"We just ran into a downdraft," he told her. "That's a small downward current of air. They aren't particularly dangerous, but they are scary. They never last more than a few seconds, though."

"A few seconds?" Trixie almost choked. "That one had to last at least five minutes!"

Bob just chuckled. "We *are* heading into more turbulence. This may turn into a rough ride. Why don't you go back with the others and have something to drink?" he suggested.

Trixie gave him no argument. Joining the other Bob-Whites for hot tea, she good-naturedly agreed when they told her they were glad Bob had taken over the controls so quickly.

"Remind me to leave town the day you learn to drive a car," Mart needled her. "Your idea of navigation leaves something to be desired." His eyes told her he admired her spirit, though.

"Bob didn't think I was that bad a pilot," Trixie defended herself.

"I notice he didn't give you back the controls," Brian chuckled.

"That's because it looks like we're heading into a storm," Trixie told him. "Anyway, I think flying's great . . . except for the downdrafts."

Jim grinned at her and spoke up. "Before we land, let's talk some more about what Dad expects of us. He sent along a little notebook and pen for each of us." He passed them out. "We're to write down anything that we notice, good or bad, immediately. He also wants us to make two lists: one of the things we like best about the place—"

"Let me guess," broke in Di. "The other is the things we like the least."

Jim nodded. "But we're not to share our lists with each other. They are to be made independently. All of our other notes will be combined into one major report that we'll give to Dad and Mr. Kimball with our recommendations. We'll also meet with both of them and some of their advisers later, so Dad said to really make sure we know what we're talking about."

"Right," said Miss Trask, gathering everyone's plastic cups and stowing them in her flight bag. "This is a case where what you think can make a lot of difference."

"Honey and I have decided that we can share the typing of the report," Jim went on. "But we'll all have to chip in when it comes to actually writing it."

"Especially Mart," Honey said warmly. "We may need words of more than one syllable."

"I don't see why," said Trixie innocently. "We don't want Mr. Wheeler to have to spend years deciphering our report."

Before Mart could respond, Miss Trask reached into her bag and pulled out some travel folders. "I thought you all might find these interesting," she said. "They're about Vermont."

"Swell," said Brian, taking one. "We Beldens have never been to Vermont."

"I did go to the library one morning before class and look Vermont up in the encyclopedia," Trixie volunteered in a smug voice.

"Undoubtedly when you should have been studying for your math final," remarked Mart.

Trixie ignored him. "The name comes from *Vert Mont,* the French words for *Green Mountain.* Vermont is nicknamed the Green Mountain State, too."

Miss Trask looked pleased. "The Green Mountains are part of the Appalachians, as are the Catskills around Sleepyside," she informed them. "The mountain scenery makes Vermont one of the most beautiful states in the country."

"I hope the mountains aren't green when we get there," Jim said lightly. "I'm counting on a little of the white stuff myself."

"Don't worry, Jim," said Miss Trask. "The Green Mountains get between eighty and one hundred twenty inches of snow every year. The skiing season's already started."

"Say," broke in Mart, "doesn't it seem like the plane is losing altitude? We must be getting close."

Sure enough, they had begun their plunge through the layers of black clouds. The little plane bounced from air current to air current as it descended into the storm.

Di grew pale. "My stomach can't take much more of this," she groaned.

"It won't have to," Honey reassured her. "I can see the runway lights now."

"Hey, look!" Trixie cried. "It's really snowing like mad. No wonder there was so much turbulence."

The plane hit the ground, bounced back up, touched

the ground again, and finally rolled to a stop. For a moment, they all stayed in their seats, taking in their first look at Groverville through the dense pattern of snow.

"At least this snow will make for good skiing tomorrow," Jim said, as Bob helped them all out of the plane.

"Sure, if it stops by then," Mart grumbled.

"Yipes," moaned Trixie. "After all this, you mean we're going to be trapped inside the lodge the whole week?"

"Oh, Trixie, don't worry," Honey laughed. "The storm will pass, probably by morning. Daddy said he made arrangements for a rental car. Let's find it."

"That must be it over there," Miss Trask said, pointing to a beige Volkswagen van parked in front of a sign reading RESERVED FOR RENTALS.

"I always thought this clan needed a tan van," quipped Mart.

"That's cute," giggled Di. She picked up a handful of snow and threw it in the direction of the car. "I hereby christen you the Tan Van."

Honey turned to Bob. "Are you coming to the lodge with us?" she asked. "Or may we drop you off somewhere?"

"I'm going to secure the plane and catch a cab to the nearest hotel. I've got to be back in town first thing tomorrow," Bob said cordially as he handed them their luggage from the plane's hold. "I'll see you next week. Have a great time, kids, and you, too, Miss Trask."

Twenty minutes later, Miss Trask was pulling off the main highway and onto the steep winding road that led to the lodge. The snow was falling harder now, making it difficult to see the road. Miss Trask, a superb driver, shifted into low gear and slowly maneuvered her way up the hill. Everyone in the car was silent, letting her concentrate on driving.

Trixie stared out her window, watching the wind swirl the snow around the trees along the side of the road. It looked so cold and unfriendly outside that she pulled her parka tighter around her and started snuggling down into the seat.

Suddenly, one of the swirls seemed to take form—the form of a human being! Trixie jerked up and pressed her face against the window. Was the wind playing tricks on her, or was there a *person* out in this awful storm?

A Dubious Welcome • 3

STOP THE CAR!" Trixie yelled.

Miss Trask began to brake, and the van swerved. "I can't stop—it's too dangerous," she said tersely. "What's the matter?"

"I—I think I saw an old woman lost in the storm."

Miss Trask sighed. "Now, Trixie, you know you have a vivid imagination."

"But I saw someone, really!"

"What exactly did you see, Trixie?" asked Jim.

"The back of a person disappearing into the woods," Trixie said. "She had all this long white hair."

"I know what you saw," said Brian matter-of-factly. "A tree stump covered with snow."

"But it moved, Brian."

"It must have been a stump, Trixie," Honey argued gently. "No one would be out in this storm."

Trixie was not convinced. "Di, did you see anything?" she demanded.

"Well, I did see some movement right before you yelled," Di replied doubtfully, "but it could have been the wind."

Miss Trask swung the van into the lodge parking area and breathed deeply. "Well, I for one am glad to be off the roads before they get any worse. Trixie, do you really think we have to go back and check out the old woman you thought you saw?"

The long day's activities were starting to take their toll on Trixie. Getting ready for the party that morning seemed like years ago. "No, Miss Trask," she murmured. "I guess not. Even if it were a woman, she'd be gone by now." She sighed and curled up on the seat. "Boy, am I tired. I could go to sleep right here."

Mart leaned over and tapped her on the head. *"Un momento,* dear sister. I don't mind carrying your luggage, but *you* most definitely are too heavy."

Trixie jumped up. "Did you hear that? He volunteered to carry my suitcase!"

"I've been had!" Mart protested.

Miss Trask pulled the van as close to the lodge as she could. While the others got their luggage out, Trixie ran for the large double doors of the lodge.

Once inside, she gazed appreciatively around the spacious lobby. Most noticeable was the towering Christmas pine tree nearly touching the peak of the cathedral ceiling. One entire wall was taken up by a large stone fireplace fenced in by comfortable-looking chairs and couches. At the other end of the room, opposite the fireplace, was the reception desk. The wall between the fireplace and the reception desk, facing the mountain, was entirely glassed in, but nothing could be seen in the outside floodlights except falling snow.

Hearing footsteps, Trixie whirled around to see a tall, muscular blond man entering the room. He was wearing a very tight striped T-shirt tucked into bell-bottom jeans, and he had a clipper ship under full sail tattooed on his left forearm. With the rope sandals on his feet, he looked like a misplaced beachcomber. *What a peculiar outfit for a ski lodge,* thought Trixie.

By this time, the others were filing into the lobby. Jim headed straight for the blond man. "Hi!" he greeted him. "Are you Pat O'Brien?"

The man extended his hand and said, "No, I'm Bert Mitchell. Pat is expecting some kind of investigating team to arrive late tonight, so he and Katie are in the kitchen making sandwiches." He held up his other hand, revealing a half-eaten sandwich. "They're good, too."

Mart grinned. "Good, because we're hungry."

"We're that investigating team," Jim explained, and then he introduced all of them.

"You? But you're just a bunch of kids!" Bert scoffed. "What do you do—watch to see who's stealing out of the cookie jar?" He grinned at his own wit.

Miss Trask stepped forward and said firmly, "Honey and Jim's father is considering buying the lodge, and he wants to know if young people like this area."

"I see," said Bert, still grinning. "You're on a sort of vacation, huh?"

"No," replied Jim evenly, "we're on a job. Could you please tell me where the kitchen is, so I can talk to Mr. O'Brien?"

"Right through the door next to the reception desk," replied Bert.

After Jim left, Bert turned to the others. "Hey, kids, I'm sorry for laughing at you. When Pat said he was getting rooms ready for some people coming to investigate the lodge, I expected Sherlock Holmes types, not people whose father wants to buy it."

"That certainly is understandable, Mr. Mitchell," said Honey pleasantly. "But we are taking our work very seriously."

"I can tell," he said, seeming impressed. "Call me Bert, by the way. How long do you plan to stay?"

"Only a week," Trixie replied.

"Well, I'm sure you'll enjoy yourselves. I'm going to hit the hay now. See you later," Bert said, and he strode off down the hall, sandals flopping.

"We should have told him about the Belden-Wheeler Detective Agency," Trixie sniffed. "Then he could have had a real laugh."

"Hey, everyone, come here," Di called. She was standing at the reception desk, looking up at a beautiful picture on the wall. It was of the sun setting on the mountains, washing a rainbow of colors over them.

"Why, that's a Stevenson print," said Miss Trask.

"Isn't it gorgeous?"

"It sure is," agreed Mart. "Who is Stevenson?"

"You mean I know something you don't?" Trixie crowed. "Carl Stevenson is only the best and most famous printmaker on the East Coast. If you'd take your nose out of the dictionary sometime, you'd learn there's more to this world than words."

"Don't you remember the reception my parents had last spring to benefit the art museum?" Di asked him. "His daughter, Ellen, was there."

"Now I remember," said Mart. "She's the one who handles the business end of his art work, because he's practically a hermit. I really like his stuff."

Just then, Jim came back into the lobby with a tall, lean, athletic man with wavy auburn hair and twinkling green eyes.

Pat O'Brien grinned infectiously as Jim completed all the introductions. "Welcome to Mead's Mountain!" he said. "I sure hope Mr. Wheeler does carry out his plan for this place. It's very special. It's been a wonderful home for Katie—that's my wife—and our little girl, Rosie." Then he sighed. "We'll be sorry to leave it."

That's funny, Trixie thought. *I thought Mr. Wheeler said the O'Briens were the* new *caretakers.*

Pat picked up Miss Trask's suitcase and said, "Katie's making sandwiches and hot chocolate for you, and I've got a fire going in the fireplace in your suite. Come on!"

When Trixie started to follow him, Mart grabbed her arm and pointed to her suitcase still sitting on the floor. "You're on your own now, toots." Trixie made a great show of struggling with her suitcase.

"Let's get you settled so you can tackle these mountains in the morning," Pat was saying as she caught up to the group. "I've put you in suite twenty-three at the end of the hall. There're two dorm rooms with bunk beds in each. Both of them open onto a small balcony overlooking the mountain. There's another bedroom for you," he told Miss Trask. "You have a small kitchen, although Mr. Wheeler said you'd be eating most of your meals in the restaurant. A sliding glass door opens out onto the pool. I think you'll enjoy it."

"I'm sure we will. It sounds very nice," Miss Trask answered.

"Especially the bed part," yawned Mart.

"Mr. O'Brien?" Trixie fell into step with him as they walked down the hall.

"Pat, please."

"Pat, on the way up here I saw some movement alongside the road. The others thought it must have been the wind, but it looked like a person to me. All I could see was the back and what looked like long white hair."

Pat just stared at her for a moment, and then he chuckled. "You're not the first person to say you've seen a figure with long white hair in these mountains, especially on nights like tonight, when the snows, winds, and imaginations are active. You mean you don't know what you saw?"

Trixie shook her head.

"The ghost of Thomas Mead, of course," Pat said,

with a tiny flicker of a smile.

Di stopped short. "You don't really believe that, do you?" she asked nervously.

"Oh, I don't know," Pat answered. "A great many people in this area do believe it. And the story makes for a lot of fun."

"To Trixie, ethereal beings are not fun; they're—" Mart, noticing the glare Trixie was giving him, decided not to continue.

At the end of the hall, Pat put down the suitcase and fumbled for his key ring. "You should have plenty of privacy in this section of the lodge," he told them. "The only other people near you are a young honeymooning couple, and we don't see them too often."

Finally he got the door open. The Bob-Whites peered in and saw what normally would have been an inviting, cozy room. In the center was a circular fireplace. Surrounding it were gold and brown overstuffed chairs. The floor was covered with a thick rust carpet, and the walnut-paneled walls were decorated with pictures of mountain scenes.

But, where the fire Pat had promised should have been, there were only ashes floating in a pool of water. And the patio door was standing wide open, allowing the wind to blow the cold air and the falling snow inside.

Pat looked genuinely distressed as he rushed over and closed the patio door. "I don't know what to say! Who could have done this?" he asked, turning helplessly to the Bob-Whites.

Trixie looked alertly around the room. "Whoever

did it just did it recently," she answered.

"How do you know?" demanded Pat.

"Well, the room is still a little warm, and there isn't that much snow on the rug."

"That's true," said Pat. "But how could they have gotten in? The door was locked."

"The patio door wasn't locked when we got here," Trixie pointed out. "Maybe it wasn't before, either."

"I didn't double-check it when I readied the room," Pat admitted, still looking dazed.

Trixie headed for the patio door, and Jim followed her. Outside the door, the snow was totally smooth except where the wind had blown it into drifts. "Hmm, no footprints. No one but a ghost could have come through this door," observed Trixie.

Then, by the glare of the floodlights, she saw something as startling as the scene in their room. "What in the world– The swimming pool is outside! Jeepers, who would want to swim outdoors in weather like this? Do you suppose they haven't finished the roof yet, Jim?"

"No, I think it's supposed to be that way. See the steam rolling off the pool? That means the water has been heated and is probably very comfortable."

"Sure, it's like a Finnish sauna," Mart informed them as he came out on the patio. "You roll in those large snowdrifts next to the pool and then jump in. Only in Finland, you jump into a natural hot spring. It's supposed to be very relaxing."

"It does sound neat," Trixie said. "I can't wait to try it in the morning."

"Right now I think you should try going into the kitchen," said Mart. "Our culprit left a calling card."

"Why didn't you tell me?" Trixie demanded, almost knocking him over in her rush to get back inside.

Trixie hurried to the corner of the main room where there was a small sink, stove, refrigerator, and breakfast counter. On the counter, written in large block letters with a bright red liquid, were the words:

LEAVE MY MOUNTAIN NOW!

T.L.M.

"Thomas L. Mead!" Trixie breathed. "So that *was* him I saw on the road—and he's *been* here!"

"Not so fast," said Mart sternly. "In the first place, it's 'that was *he* I saw on the road.' In the second place, what you saw was a stump. The real truth is that someone is playing a practical joke on us."

Trixie was about to make a furious reply, when there was a knock on the door.

Pat looked startled. "I don't know what to expect around here anymore," he said, going to answer the door.

It was a young man of about twenty, carrying a tray of sandwiches and mugs of hot chocolate.

"Oh, it's Eric." Pat sighed in relief. "Wait till you see this mess. Eric works here," Pat told the others.

Eric was long-limbed and lean, with very curly, longish blond hair and watery blue eyes. As Pat made the introductions, Eric passed around the tray and gave each of them a wide smile, revealing perfectly straight white teeth.

Eric seemed as baffled as Pat by the intrusion and the message on the counter. He touched the red liquid with his finger and then put it to his tongue. "Catsup," he announced.

"Oh," quivered Di. "I was sure it was blood."

"Someone is trying to be funny," Pat said, trying to sound calm. "It's my fault for forgetting to lock the patio door. I can assure you it won't happen again. I'm off to tell Katie about this. Good night, everyone."

Eric quickly cleaned up the fireplace and the counter, and then he, too, said good night.

As she locked the door after them, Miss Trask commented, "I can't imagine anyone doing such a peculiar thing."

"Neither can I," said Brian, taking out his notebook. "But I'll tell you, this lodge does not rate high on warm welcomes."

"What do you make of it, Trixie?" Jim asked.

"I'm not really sure," she answered. "But I think that ghostly person I saw on the road may be connected to this somehow."

"Trixie," Mart began, finishing the last of his hot chocolate, "just because you choose to believe in exteriorized protoplasm does *not* mean you have to foist your hallucinations on us."

"I don't know what you're talking about," said Trixie, her eyes flashing. "All I know is that there were no footprints outside that patio door. And someone, or something, wants to scare us away from Mead's Mountain!"

"Trixie, we can't be sure of that at all," Miss Trask

tried to reason with her. "I tend to agree with Mart. Someone is playing a practical joke, and it's in extremely poor taste. Right now I think we'd better get some sleep. We have a long day behind us and a big day ahead of us."

Even Trixie had to agree.

Locked Doors, Missing Quarters • 4

DESPITE THE LATENESS of their bedtime, the Bob-Whites awoke early the following morning, excited about the week of mountain adventure ahead. It was a beautiful day. The snow had stopped, and the sun was shining its warmest possible welcome.

Now, this *is the way to start a mountain vacation,* Trixie thought.

The first thing on the agenda was an early morning swim. Trixie, Honey, and Di threw towels over their swimsuits and, not bothering to put shoes on, stepped outside the sliding glass door. A chilly gust of mountain air sent them hopping on their toes toward the pool as fast as they could go. Wasting no time, they jumped into the soothing warm water, where the boys had already started their swim.

"Mmmm. . . . This is gorgeous!" Di purred. "It's just like taking a bath outside!"

"Not quite!" hollered Jim as he scrambled out of the pool. At the pool's edge, the boys had made an arsenal of snowballs, which they now used to bombard the girls.

Laughing and screaming, the girls kept diving under the water. As long as they could stay underwater, they were safe. Whenever they came up for air, they found themselves all too visible targets.

Finally the boys could stand the cold air no longer and were forced to jump back into the pool. The girls delighted in taking their revenge by dunking the boys thoroughly and repeatedly. Honey challenged each of the boys to a race and won easily each time.

Floating lazily in the shallow end, Di announced that she had to get out so she could get her hair dry before breakfast.

"Excellent timing," said Mart. "You damsels go try to beautify yourselves, a task, which, although feasible for Di and Honey, will be impossible for Trixie. By the time we he-men get out, you can be cleared out of the bathroom."

"By the time you he-men get out, you'll be as wrinkled as prunes," said Trixie saucily, "which, I must say, will greatly improve your looks."

Clutching their towels around them, the girls darted to the sliding glass door, and Trixie tugged on it. It didn't move.

"It's locked!" she gasped.

"Oh, no!" Honey trembled, hopping from one cold foot to another. "We're covered with goose bumps. Pound on the door, Trixie. Maybe Miss Trask will hear."

Trixie thumped on the door, but Miss Trask had apparently left for breakfast. "I guess we'll have to make a run for the hallway door," she quavered.

"What if that one is locked, too?" worried Di as they started running.

"There's got to be an unlocked door around here somewhere," answered Trixie. "I'll bet anything this is Mart's idea of a cute trick. He probably locked the door, and that's why he was so generous about letting us have the bathroom first."

"Y-You don't think it could have been the 'ghost' again, do you, Trixie?" asked Di apprehensively.

That thought had already occurred to Trixie, but to reassure Di she said, "Actually, we probably locked it ourselves accidentally. I guess it couldn't have been Mart after all. He was with us the whole time."

The girls cheered breathlessly when they found the hallway door open. Once in the hall, they stopped running, but it was hard to stop shivering. As they rounded the corner that led to their suite, they almost ran right into Eric.

"What are you doing here?" Trixie demanded, her teeth still chattering.

"I–I was looking for Rosie," he said, staring at the girls. "She said she was going to visit you, but she's not there. You girls shouldn't be running around in weather like this in those wet bathing suits. You could freeze to death. I didn't think you were that dumb."

Trixie looked Eric right in the eye. "Someone locked our patio door that opens out onto the pool."

Eric just shrugged and walked away.

Di ran ahead and tried their door. "Hurray!" she yelled. "First dibs on the shower!"

While Honey and Trixie waited their turns, Honey said, "Trixie, don't you think you were kind of rude? Why, the way you looked at him, you were practically accusing him of locking our door."

"Well, he called us dumb for getting locked out," Trixie said defensively. She knew she tended to jump to conclusions.

Trixie went over to examine the lock on the patio door. "This isn't the kind of lock you can accidentally lock," she announced. "Someone must have locked it from the inside."

"It must have been that practical joker," said Honey. "I don't like this, Trixie. You don't really believe there is a 'ghost' who doesn't want Daddy to buy the lodge, do you?"

"Of course not. Nobody else really believes it, either. But if a person is playing ghost, I'd sure like to figure out how and why."

"Why can't we ever go anywhere without strange things happening?" Honey sighed. "Trixie, *why* are you grinning? There's nothing funny about this!"

"I know," Trixie said honestly. "I just—well, when your father started telling us about the ghost, well, I was kind of hoping for some excitement."

"Well, I think you're getting more than you bargained for," Honey cautioned. "Come on, let's get ready for breakfast."

Trixie's short curls dried much faster than the shoulder-length cuts of Di and Honey, so she decided to meet the others in the restaurant later. She thought she would take a walk before breakfast and see more of Mead's Mountain.

When she stepped out into the hall, she saw a young couple coming toward her, arm in arm. He was tall and slim, with smooth, dark skin and long, black hair. She was shorter, but slim and dark, too. Her hair was pulled back and piled on her head, and her features were delicate and finely chiseled. Whispering and flashing smiles to each other, they stopped at the door next to the Bob-Whites' suite.

"Good morning," Trixie greeted them and introduced herself. "We're staying in the suite next to you. If we make too much noise, just bang on the wall."

They smiled and introduced themselves as Mr. and Mrs. Allessi. "Welcome," said the woman. "Don't worry about bothering us."

"Have a good day on the slopes," said the man as they disappeared into their room.

Honeymooners are lovely people, thought Trixie as she walked down the hall. Once she got outside in the courtyard, she took a deep breath of mountain air and gazed at the beautiful scenery around her.

The lodge was situated in a hollow at the base of a string of mountains, and it was much larger than it had looked the previous night. The way its Alpine styling was silhouetted against the mountains almost convinced Trixie that she must be in a mountain meadow in Switzerland. She guessed that the largest peak in the chain of mountains must be Mead's Mountain. Except for the mountains, most of the land Trixie could see around the lodge was gently sloping, forested hills.

The main lobby and restaurant faced the mountains, showing off the spectacular view. Connected to the main building, and housing the guest rooms, was a rectangular building with the open courtyard in the center, where the swimming pool was located. A breezeway passed through the center of the courtyard, and Trixie followed it, marveling at how the sun made everything snow-covered shine like diamonds. Coming around to the front of the main lodge, she could see a bunny tow and a more advanced rope tow meet the start of the chair lift. She was looking forward to learning how to cross-country ski.

Tromping through snowdrifts and breathing the invigorating air was making her hungry, so Trixie headed for the restaurant. None of the others were there yet, and she decided to wait outside the front entrance. She brushed the snow off a small bench in the sunshine and sat down. Soon engrossed in scribbling down her impressions of the lodge area into her notebook, she was startled when Jim sat down next to her.

"Good morning," he said. "And *what* a morning—just smell that air!" He took an extremely deep breath and started to slowly let it out.

Sounds of crashing glass and a small child's shrill

scream cut short his exhale. Jim leaped up and went inside, Trixie close at his heels. He came to a halt just inside the door, and Trixie, unable to stop, bumped right into him. It had been so bright outside that at first she couldn't see a thing except spots. When her eyes adjusted, she was horrified to see a small, barefoot girl about five years old, standing amid the debris of a broken peanut butter jar.

"Don't move," Jim ordered, slowly approaching the girl. The little girl, taken by surprise, stood perfectly still and quit crying.

"I broke my peanut butter," she sniffed. "That's my most favorite thing of all."

Jim gingerly stepped into the mess, picked up the girl, and carried her to a table. Trixie watched him examine the girl's feet for cuts and thought, *Jim is so good and tender with small children.* In a few minutes, Jim had the curly-haired girl laughing.

"You won't tell my mama, will you? I'm supposed to be in bed," she pleaded, pointing to her pajamas.

Just then a lovely woman with thick black braids and wearing a floor-length skirt came rushing into the room. Behind her was Miss Trask.

"Rosie, I told you to stay in bed. What are you doing in here?" the woman scolded, gathering the girl into her arms.

Rosie burst into tears again and wailed, "I broke the peanut butter. I got hungry and I broke the peanut butter."

"Oh, Rosie, how many times have I told you not to take things that don't belong to you? You know you're not supposed to get into the pantry."

This additional scolding only brought more tears.

"You're very lucky, honey, because I just happen to have another jar of peanut butter in the pantry," the woman said soothingly. "Now, let's see if you're okay."

"That man said I was okay. He saved me," Rosie sniffed solemnly. She pointed to Jim, causing Jim's face to turn the same shade of red as his hair.

The woman stepped forward, extending her hand to Jim. "I'm Katie O'Brien," she said warmly. "I'm grateful to you for tending to my very disobedient daughter," she added, giving Rosie a reproachful look.

"As my friend Mart would say, helping out damsels in distress is my specialty," Jim managed to respond. He patted Rosie's tangled dark curls and introduced himself and Trixie.

"Miss Trask and my husband, Pat, have been telling me about you. I'm glad to be able to match names with faces." Katie set Rosie down on the floor and gave her a gentle pat. "Now, Rosie, off to the apartment with you. Daddy's still there. He'll help you get dressed." She turned to Trixie, Jim, and Miss Trask. "I'll get this mess cleaned up and fix your breakfast. Then we can talk." She sighed, looking around at the peanut butter rubble.

"I'll clean it up," Jim offered. Before Katie could object, Jim heard the rest of the Bob-Whites coming in. "Miss Trask, would you introduce everyone while I go get a mop and some paper towels?"

By the time Jim joined the others in the dining

area, the Bob-Whites and Katie were talking as if they were old friends.

"My blood sugar is at a low ebb, and I crave solid sustenance. Might I suggest we procure the house cuisine?" Mart requested politely.

Katie gave him a puzzled stare.

"Mart's got this disease called dictionary-itis," Trixie tried to explain. "I think he means he's hungry."

Katie smiled approvingly. "I love a boy with an appetite. Is there anything special you'd like?"

"Bacon and scrambled eggs?" Jim suggested.

"How about adding hashbrowns, toast, and juice?" Mart put in quickly. "Mountain air, you know."

Miss Trask laughed. "Katie, I'm afraid you'll get to know Mart's appetite all too well by the end of the week."

Katie disappeared into the kitchen, and the Bob-Whites and Miss Trask sat down at one of the long tables covered with a bright tablecloth. In came a petite, brown-haired girl carrying a tray of mugs of steaming hot chocolate.

With a friendly smile, she introduced herself as Linda Fleming. "Katie thought you might want some hot chocolate after your early morning swim. How do you like the pool?" she asked, passing around the tray.

"What a way to start the day!" Brian rhapsodized.

"You just liked it because you were able to swim and have a snowball fight at the same time," said Trixie sourly.

"And *you*, Beatrix, are just mad because you kept

forgetting to duck," chuckled Mart.

"Just wait till later. You'll get yours," threatened Trixie, pretending to throw a snowball.

"You certainly know how to strike terror into the heart of a young boy," Mart said, not bothering to duck.

"Don't mind them," Brian told Linda. "They're still going through sibling rivalry. I take it you work here?"

"Yes, with my twin sister, Wanda. We're taking a semester off from college to earn money for expenses. Since we love to ski, working here is really ideal for us. Here comes Wanda now." She pointed to a girl coming toward them with another tray.

Wanda was a little taller than her sister and had a sturdier build. She had long dark hair that flowed all the way down her back and, like her sister, had the healthy, glowing complexion that goes with outdoor living.

"This is only the beginning," Wanda said cheerfully as she passed around the large pottery bowls of scrambled eggs and hashbrowns and the platter of bacon.

"Wow! Food service wins the prize for high ratings," said Mart. Before he even took a bite, he took out his notebook and quickly scribbled down a few words.

Di looked knowing. "I can guess what's on Mart's like list."

"Just wait till you taste the food," mumbled Mart between mouthfuls. "It will end up on yours, too."

"Pat told us about your father's plan for this lodge,"

said Wanda to Honey and Jim. "Linda and I are delighted. We grew up in Groverville and have been coming to these mountains since we were little kids. We have a lot of memories of fishing and camping with our parents here, and we were hoping this wouldn't be turned into a large commercial ski area. It's hard to find this kind of solitude, freedom, and peacefulness anywhere else, so it would be a terrible waste to ruin the area with another ski resort. Vermont has so many."

"This does seem like the ideal place for a natural resort area," Jim agreed.

"Mead's Mountain is a private, personal kind of place," Linda said emotionally. "I know in the week you're here you'll get to love it the way Wanda and I do."

Katie came in with still another tray, this one with big pitchers of orange juice and milk and baskets of homemade sweet rolls.

"Katie," Honey said, looking at her appreciatively, "I'm surprised to see you in a long skirt, instead of in ski pants like Linda and Wanda. Don't you like to ski?"

"Honey, I'll let you in on my secret." Katie lifted her gaily colored skirt to her knees, revealing a pair of ski pants underneath. "I love to ski! I'd rather ski than just about anything, but I do have other duties. When I'm just wearing ski pants, I want to be out on the slopes, but somehow in a long skirt I feel more like an indoor-type pioneer woman. So I wear the skirt while I work inside, but I keep the ski clothes on underneath so I'll be ready to go instantly."

"How clever," said Trixie, glad that she herself hardly ever had to wear a long skirt.

There were no other people in the restaurant yet, so Katie sat down with the group. "Tell me more about yourselves," she requested. "What do you do? What are your plans for the future?"

"Well, we're all outdoors people," Jim began, "so I know we'll enjoy our time here."

"Someday Jim's going to have a school for orphan boys, where lessons will be sandwiched in between outdoor activities," Di put in. "I myself am interested in art."

"And Brian's going to be Jim's doctor in residence," Honey contributed.

"If I ever make it through medical school," Brian commented. "I also hope to serve in a medical program—like the ship HOPE. Mart here is going to be Jim's agriculturist in residence."

"Trixie and Honey plan to operate the Belden-Wheeler Detective Agency when they get out of college," Mart said, helping himself to his third sweet roll. Then he winked. "They think they're professionals already, so we, uh, try to humor them. If you have any mysteries lying around—beware!"

"Detectives?" Katie raised an eyebrow.

Di, always loyal, jumped to the girls' defense. "Trixie and Honey are every bit as good as professionals. They've solved lots of cases when even the police were stumped, and they've made a lot of people happy, me included."

"What do *you* say, Miss Trask?" Katie asked.

"It's quite true," replied Miss Trask. "But let's save the stories of their exploits for another time."

"Please do," said Katie, glancing up at the new arrivals coming into the restaurant. She excused herself and hurried back to the kitchen.

"If you're such great detectives," said Wanda somewhat skeptically, "maybe you can find my missing quarters."

Mart pointed at Wanda. "Quiet, ye doubting Thomas, or ye will stir up a hornet's nest."

Trixie was instantly alert. "Missing quarters?"

"Whenever I have a few quarters in change, I put them in the jar on my desk," explained Wanda. "When the jar is full, I take them down to the bank and put them into my buy-a-car-someday fund. The jar was almost full."

"When did you notice it was missing?" Trixie asked.

"Let's see . . . the day before Christmas Eve. I had just shown Eric—that's our new ski instructor—to his room. I went to tell Katie that he was here, and when I came back, the jar was gone. I didn't keep my door locked then, so anyone could have taken it."

"Does Eric spend a lot of quarters?" asked Trixie thoughtfully.

Wanda shrugged. "I don't know."

"As you can see, Wanda, Trixie's more of a professional jumper-to-conclusions than a detective," Mart scoffed. "Come on, everyone. We came here to ski!"

"You came to the right place," said Linda. "I'll go help you with your skis, and then Eric can give you lessons. He's an expert cross-country skier. He's out packing down snow on the bunny tow right now."

"Very crafty." Wanda grinned at her sister. "That leaves me with the dirty dishes."

"I owe you one," called Linda, already out the door.

"See you at lunch, Miss Trask," Honey said as the Bob-Whites followed Linda to the ski shop.

While Linda was outfitting them with the narrow lightweight skis, Trixie asked casually, "Was Eric just hired a couple of days ago?"

Linda nodded. "Eric and his mother had reservations for two weeks during the Christmas holidays. Pat was surprised when Eric arrived alone and asked him for a job. Luckily for Eric, things were much busier here than Pat had anticipated, and he really needed some extra help, both on the slopes and around the lodge."

"I wonder what happened to his mother," Trixie mused aloud. At Mart's warning look, she stopped talking. But she couldn't stop thinking. *And why would he show up alone at Christmastime? Most people have something better to do than get a new job.*

Impatient, she grabbed her skis and said, "Come on, we've got a ski lesson waiting for us."

Mart sighed. "I have a feeling Eric has a barrage of questions waiting for him," he muttered to himself.

A Ski Lesson • 5

LINDA LED THEM to the base of the hill where the two rope tows converged below the chair lift. Before going back to the restaurant, she called to Eric, and he skied over to them, smiling.

There're those perfect teeth again, Trixie thought. She tried to be objective as she studied him. In his blue jeans and dark red bulky hand-knit sweater, he had a confident, casual air. Then why should watching him make her feel slightly uneasy?

"Greetings," he said. "Something tells me that none of you have ever cross-country skied."

"We're eager to learn, though," said Jim.

"And we all know how to downhill ski," added Honey quickly.

"Well, then you've got it made," Eric said. "I guarantee you'll all be near-experts in an hour. Let's go over to that flat place on the other side of this run. You can put your skis on there, and it's a good place to get the hang of the glide-kick movement."

As the Bob-Whites did as they were told, Trixie tried to get Eric to reveal more about himself. "Linda was just telling us that your mother had reservations to come here, too," she said as nonchalantly as she could. "It's too bad she changed her mind. This is such a lovely place to spend the Christmas holidays."

Eric shrugged. "I was sent word that she had to go on a business trip. No explanations, just a message that said she was already gone."

"You haven't heard from her at all?" asked Trixie, glad that Eric wasn't as reluctant to talk as she thought he'd be.

"Nope. Shortly before Christmas, my grandfather sent me a telegram saying Mom had been called away on a business trip to the West Coast and I was to stay at school for the holidays. I didn't hear a word from Mom. She usually tells me where she's going to be." He sounded hurt. "Anyway, I wasn't about to stay at school all alone, so I came here hoping to get a job to earn my keep. I was lucky—teaching skiing is like not working at all."

"Didn't you try to get in touch with your mother?" Brian asked, curious.

"Yeah, but no one was home, and when I called my grandfather, he said he didn't know exactly where she was—just someplace on the West Coast. And he was plenty mad I didn't stay at school, too."

"Maybe her business won't take long," Honey tried to console him. "Then she'll be able to join you here. Did you leave word at your school where she could find you?"

Eric nodded glumly. "I don't know too much about business, but Christmas seems like a lousy time to conduct it. I'm majoring in architecture myself. Something I'd really like to do is build ski lodges. That would rank right up there with giving ski lessons as being more fun than work! Speaking of lessons, we'd better get started."

As the Bob-Whites put on their skis, Eric explained the equipment. "As you've noticed, the boots are really just leather tennis shoes," he said, helping Di with her skis. "You want as little weight as possible. Since cross-country skiing can be quite strenuous, there's no sense expending extra energy by overloading yourself. I'm glad to see you're all wearing lightweight clothing." He gave Di, in her royal purple knickers and lavender Nordic ski sweater, an approving nod.

Di seems to turn heads everywhere we go, thought Trixie affectionately.

Eric held his leg straight out so his ski was standing on end. "The skis are long and narrow for gliding, and they don't have the sharp edges for turning, like downhill skis do. So, avoid any trees long before you come to them!"

Then Eric demonstrated the gliding gait basic to cross-country skiing. In a very short time, all the

Bob-Whites had mastered it. Trixie couldn't help feeling disappointed. *If cross-country skiing is just shuffling around on flat places in the snow, then it's not a sport I could get very excited about,* she thought.

As if he were reading her mind, Eric assured them, "It may seem a bit boring now, but once you learn to run uphill on the skis, you'll really start to enjoy cross-country."

"Run uphill on skis! You must be kidding!" said Di, her violet eyes opening wide.

Eric smiled. "It's not that hard. That's why waxing the bottom of your skis is so important. It helps you stick to the snow when you're going uphill."

"But how about coming back down the hill? Don't you stick then, too?" worried Trixie.

"No, friction from the speed of going downhill melts off the snow sticking to the wax. Some skis have commercial finishes so you don't have to wax, but we purists prefer to wax. That way you can get the best finish for the day's weather conditions. Besides, waxing is almost a ritual. Linda helped you wax already, didn't she?"

"Yes," Jim answered. "She said to tell you she had us put on green wax. Is that right?"

"Green's a good choice for today with the new snow and perfect sunny weather. Since you're new to the sport, though, maybe we should add a blue kicker."

"A blue what?" asked Trixie.

"Sounds like an illegal drug," commented Mart.

"A blue kicker—that's an extra layer of wax right underneath the boot area. It gives a bit of added grip going up hills," Eric explained.

"Well, I'm all for that," said Trixie, grinning.

Eric demonstrated how to run uphill, and then how to herringbone up steeper grades by placing skis in a V-shape, leaning forward, and waddling uphill like a duck. He made it all look easy, but the Bob-Whites soon discovered how deceiving looks could be. The first few times they tried running uphill, they found themselves slipping backward instead. When herringboning, they were inclined to trip themselves up by getting their skis crossed behind them.

Just when they felt that they were finally getting their skis under control, little Rosie came skiing downhill at a breakneck speed, traveled all the way around the Bob-Whites, and quickly ran back up the hill until she was standing right over them.

"Hi!" she said, not the least bit out of breath. With her black curls peeking out from under her pink stocking cap, her cheeks flushed bright red, and her blue eyes shining innocently, Rosie looked more like a Kewpie doll than an expert skier showing up people three times her age.

"Who let that kid on the slopes?" Mart demanded. "She's a menace to my morale."

Eric chuckled. "Rosie's going to be vying for my job soon. It will be a while before you kids have her control and speed."

"I'm going to take Miss Trask for a walk," announced Rosie. "She told me to tell you we might not be here when you're ready for lunch, so you can go ahead and eat if you want."

"Have a good walk, Rosie," called Honey, as Rosie took off again at top speed.

Mart dug his ski into the snow. "Well, I'll bet I have a bigger vocabulary than she does."

"Sure, but she can probably spell better than you," teased Trixie.

"What's next, Eric?" asked Honey.

"Now you're ready to take off on your own." He hesitated, then said, "Mead's Mountain is really special. Your first experience should be a dramatic one. I think the most exciting thing would be for you to take the chair lift to the top. From there, you'll have quite a climb through the trees to get over the crest. It won't be an easy climb for you beginners, but it's worth it. When you get to the top, take one of the trails off to your right. You should have a super time in the fresh snow we got last night."

"Are there any paths up there," asked Jim, "or do we forge our own?"

"The whole state of Vermont is honeycombed with trails and paths," said Eric. "Old Indian trails, animal paths, hiking trails. Even the Appalachian National Scenic Trail isn't too far from here."

"What's that?" asked Di.

"It's a hiking trail that extends the length of the Appalachian Mountains, almost two thousand miles," explained Eric. "I've skied on it in Massachusetts, where I go to school, and I hiked on it through the Shenandoah Valley one summer. Someday I'd like to travel the entire length. I understand there's another trail that runs the length of Vermont, from Massachusetts to Canada, called the Long Trail."

"Somehow I don't think we're ready to tackle the Long Trail today," Jim said. "But it sounds like we shouldn't have any problems. First we have to go inside to get our survival kits and some snacks for a rest stop. We don't go anywhere without our kits," he told Eric.

"Good policy," said Eric. "These mountains are rough, you know. Weather can change at any time, putting someone who isn't prepared in a very dangerous position. And there's the danger of rockslides and avalanches."

"You're not making these mountains sound very inviting," Di fretted.

Eric laughed. "As long as you have your survival kits, you don't have to worry that much. What do you carry in them?"

"First aid things like different types of bandages and smelling salts," Brian answered. "Also windproof blankets, matches, compass, signal mirror, whistle, rope, flashlight . . . let's see, what else . . . oh, a can of Sterno fuel, and some dried soup mixes and tea, too, among other things."

Eric looked impressed. "Sounds like you know how to take care of yourselves in the woods. I'll see you tonight and find out how you managed. Right now, I'd better get back and help Pat. Good luck!"

The Bob-Whites skied back down the hill to the lodge. "It feels nice to be going downhill for a change," Honey sighed.

The girls went to the suite to get the survival kits

and to rest for a few minutes. Honey was standing in front of the dresser, looking into the mirror to put on lip balm, when suddenly she gasped.

"It's gone! Trixie! Di! My watch is gone! I put it right here on the dresser before we went to bed last night. I know I did. Ohhhh!" She sank onto the bottom bunk.

"Jeepers, Honey, what are you talking about?" asked Trixie.

"My good gold watch. The one that belonged to my grandmother. She gave it to my mother when she finished school, and Mother gave it to me when I was so sick, before we came to Manor House. It's very old and very valuable!"

"Don't worry, Honey," said Di, sitting down on the bunk and putting her arm around her friend. "We'll find it. We'll look everywhere. How can we *not* find it with a super detective like Trixie on the job?"

Trixie was already down on her hands and knees, looking under the dresser. "Not here," she said anxiously. "Move your feet, so I can check under the bed. . . . Not here, either."

They looked everywhere. In all the rooms, in all their clothing, in everyone's shoes. Soon the boys came back with snacks from the restaurant and joined the search. Everyone had just about given up, when Trixie thought of one last place to look. She got a flashlight and a knife to check in the crevice between the mirror and the dresser. No watch.

Honey's hopeful look turned to despair. "It's gone

forever! I'll never see it again," she wailed, pacing the room.

"I don't know why you brought such an expensive watch here in the first place," scolded Mart.

"I didn't mean to, Mart. I wore it to your open house, and then we were in such a hurry to catch the plane, I forgot to take it off. I didn't even notice I was still wearing it until last night, as we were going to bed."

Jim brightened. "Honey, you know how Miss Trask is always reminding you to be more careful with your things and is always picking up after you? She probably has it for safekeeping."

"Oh, Jim! Of course you're right. I'm sure she has it. Oh, I feel so much better." Honey sat down on the couch and smiled for the first time in what seemed like hours.

"I'll go ask her if she has it," volunteered Di, "just to make sure."

"You can't," said Trixie, "remember? Rosie was taking her for a walk. They could be anyplace."

"Then why don't we have lunch now?" Brian suggested. "It's almost time anyway. She may come back by the time we're done."

"A meritorious notion," cheered Mart. "Why didn't I think of that?"

"I'm amazed you didn't," Trixie sniffed.

Minutes later, the Bob-Whites were feasting on homemade split pea soup and brown bread. Bert Mitchell and another man sauntered over to their table. Bert was still dressed as oddly as he had been the previous night, Trixie noticed. The other man's outfit wasn't very typical of a ski lodge, either.

"I want you to meet my friend, Jack Caridiff," said Bert. "Do you mind if we join you?"

"Not at all," said Jim, scooting down the bench to make more room.

Jack Caridiff was short, and his striped T-shirt revealed that he had broad muscular shoulders and long hairy arms. With his ruddy complexion and his curly reddish brown hair cut close to his head, he rather reminded Trixie of a playful monkey at the zoo.

Honey, always polite, had no trouble starting a conversation with anyone, even when she was upset about something like losing a valuable heirloom. "Tell me, Bert, are you and Jack from this area?" she inquired pleasantly.

"No, not at all," Bert answered with a wink. "You might say Jack and I are from all over. We belong to the merchant marines and travel the world on tramp steamers."

"How exciting!" Trixie exclaimed immediately. The idea of sailing from port to port on a tramp steamer, taking cargo wherever it was needed, appealed to her lively sense of adventure.

"It's an interesting life," Jack agreed. "But it's nice to get away from the sea once in a while, too. A ski vacation in the mountains is our idea of excitement."

"You both ski?" Di frowned. "I didn't know sailors could ski."

"Sailors are just like other people," Jack informed her. "Some can ski, some can't. Bert and I were raised in Washington State. There's a lot of good skiing out there."

"How about swimming?" asked Mart. "Do you fit the stereotype of the sailor who loves the sea but can't swim?"

Bert chuckled. "I'm a fairly good swimmer, but Jack here refuses to fill a bathtub more than three inches."

Jack turned a shade redder than his normal red. "Aw, come off it. I just never got the hang of swimming, that's all," he said weakly.

Katie came around to their table, offering second helpings of brown bread. "Bert and Jack," she said cordially, "I see you've met our junior detectives." There was a hint of laughter in her voice.

"What do you mean?" asked Jack, looking up from his bread to Katie.

"I don't really know the whole story myself, but apparently Trixie and Honey are amateur sleuths. Isn't that right, Trixie?"

Trixie sighed. She really didn't like going into her plans for the future when she suspected that adults were laughing at her.

Honey came to her rescue. "Yes, we're going to open the Belden-Wheeler Detective Agency officially once we're out of college."

"So, you really *are* the Sherlock Holmes types, after all," teased Bert.

"Oh," said Jack, "you mean that's what you want to be when you grow up." He leaned across the table and patted Trixie's hand. "Well, don't give up your dream, kid. When I was young, I dreamed of going to sea, and look at me now—I'm a sailor."

The other Bob-Whites, sensing the adults' condescending manner, jumped to Trixie and Honey's defense. "This isn't just a dream," argued Mart. "They've solved a lot of very tough cases already. Maybe you read in the paper about the capture of an international jewel-theft organization. Trixie was responsible for that."

This announcement brought a look of sisterly affection from Trixie, but only further grins from the three adults.

"How nice," said Bert politely.

"Well, how about those people who were stockpiling guns?" added Jim, his well-known temper starting to flare. "They were going to start a revolution in South America, but Trixie figured out a coded map and helped the police capture the criminals."

Bert looked startled and put his elbows up on the table. "You're not talking about those big arsenals the FBI found on the Mississippi River, are you?" he inquired sharply.

"That was our Trixie in action," Di said proudly.

"I remember reading in the paper that a bunch of teen-agers were instrumental in helping the police," Bert said thoughtfully. "That was you kids?"

"Well, it was mostly Trixie," Brian said. "She gets the rest of us involved sooner or later."

"I guess you really do know what you're doing, Trixie," Bert admitted, leaning back again.

Trixie blushed with pleasure, more because of her

friends' support than because the adults were now convinced.

"Real detectives on Mead's Mountain," mused Katie, shaking her head. "I'll have to tell Pat about this. Maybe you can solve the mystery of Thomas Mead's ghost!"

Trixie was dying to ask her more about the ghost, but before she could formulate a question, Katie had moved on and Honey was talking.

"It's getting late," Honey was saying. "Why don't we go skiing now? We can get my watch from Miss Trask this evening."

"Sure, if that's okay with you," Jim said. "I know what that watch means to you."

"I don't mind at all," Honey answered. "Now that I'm sure that Miss Trask has it, I won't worry."

Trixie said nothing. She was remembering the previous night's prank and the locked patio door, and suddenly she wasn't at all sure that Miss Trask had that watch.

A Cabin in the Woods • 6

As Eric had instructed, the Bob-Whites began their afternoon adventure with a ride to the top of the mountain in the chair lift. When they got off, they were greeted by a large white sign with black lettering that warned THESE MOUNTAINS CAN BE DANGEROUS. WATCH FOR FALLING ROCKS AND AVALANCHES. BE PREPARED AGAINST FROSTBITE AND HYPOTHERMIA.

"How cheery," said Di. "What's hypothermia?"

"That's when exposure to cold causes body temperature to drop below normal," Jim replied. "And the warning's important, Di. Far too many people venture into the woods totally unprepared, without knowing the first thing about survival techniques."

"That doesn't mean the sign has to be worded so

as to induce an instant heart attack," Mart joked.

Between them and the crest of the mountain lay a hundred yards of heavily wooded hillside, with one small trail spiraling out of sight. The trail looked like nothing they had practiced on. In fact, it appeared to go almost straight up—a very difficult, if not impossible, climb.

"I didn't bargain for this," said Brian, staring up at the trail. "What is Eric doing—sending us on a suicide mission?"

"I don't think I'm going to like cross-country skiing," said Di apprehensively.

"Come on, you know we can do it." Jim tried to sound encouraging. "Look at the challenge! Besides, I don't think Eric would have sent us here if he didn't think we could handle it."

"I suppose you're right," agreed Honey, somewhat dubiously.

"I guess the best thing to do now is to start," Trixie determined.

"Right," said Jim. "Trixie, let's you and I lead the way and make a path in the new snow for the others."

Trixie and Jim started up the hill, then Mart followed. Next came Brian, behind him Di, and lastly, Honey.

Travel was slow and rough. Their skis kept slipping. Trixie was surprised at how fast her energy disappeared. She wasn't sure she could make the climb to the ridge after all. Somehow she kept going, summoning up hidden reserves of energy rather than admit out loud that she would just as soon turn back and forget the whole thing. It was comforting to hear Jim keep calling out words of encouragement. *How can he do that?* she thought. *How can he keep going and encourage us at the same time? I just want to drop dead.*

Suddenly Jim yelled, "I'm at the top!"

Once again Trixie found new strength. In a few seconds, she, too, reached the small plateau on top of the mountain crest. Exhausted, she dropped down next to Jim. "We did it! Victory!" she puffed.

Jim shook her hand. "The first thing that has to be done, if Dad is going to buy this place, is to extend the ski lift through those trees. Only people in top physical condition are going to make it to the top." Jim struggled to pull his notebook out of his pocket as the other Bob-Whites made it up to the small plateau and flopped down next to them.

After a few minutes of well-earned rest, Trixie pushed her sunglasses back on her head and looked around for the first time. In every direction were brilliant white peaks silhouetted against a turquoise sky. Dotting the mountains were thousands of trees—tall evergreens reaching for the sky, skeletal maples resting for the winter, birches, beeches, cedars.

It was an awesome sight. "Jeepers, we're on top of the world!" she gasped.

"I honestly didn't know there were so many mountains in the world," Honey breathed.

Down in front of them was the chair lift, a mere thread connecting them with the miniature lodge below. They could see the Tan Van, looking more like a toy, and the swimming pool, resembling the jeweled setting in a ring. Beyond the lodge was the village of Groverville, pavement ribbons extending from it.

"It's as though we've been miniaturized and placed on top of a relief map," Trixie mused.

"No," Mart disputed gently, "we're the giants. It's the rest of the world that's lilliputian."

Then, for a long time, no one spoke or moved. It was a beautiful, quiet moment. Working so hard to achieve it had made it even more special.

Presently, Jim said softly, "Shall we pick out our ski trail now?"

"Gee," Brian said, "I feel almost like an intruder."

"What say we intrude upon our snacks first?" pleaded Mart. "They must be getting lonely in our knapsacks."

The others, laughing, agreed that some nourishment was in order and got out the snacks the boys had packed earlier.

Afterward, Trixie stood up and looked around. She was ready for adventure. The thrill of exploring the unknown was coursing through her veins. "Let's take this trail," she said, pointing left. "It stays on top of the crest and winds through the trees."

"But didn't Eric say to take one of the trails to the right?" Di asked.

"Yes," recalled Trixie, "but which way is right? If you face the lodge, it's this way. But if you face the valley between us and those peaks, it's that way."

"I don't know what he meant either," said Honey. "What should we do?"

"I think Robert Frost could answer that question for us," said Mart.

"Huh?" Di looked blank.

" 'Two roads diverged in a wood, and I—I took the one less traveled by,' " he quoted.

" 'And that has made all the difference,' " Trixie finished.

"Isn't that from 'The Road Not Taken'? Since when did you become the poetry expert, Trixie?" Jim teased.

"I'm not," she admitted. "I just remember Dad reading the stuff to us when we were little, instead of bedtime stories."

"Well, none of these trails look traveled by to me," said Di, confused.

"How about this one?" Jim said. He glided over to a trail smaller and less noticeable than the others.

"Perfect!" Trixie was delighted. "That looks like our very own secret hidden trail!"

"It won't be too secret after our ski tracks are left behind," Mart pointed out, getting ready to follow Jim.

"It looks fun, though," said Brian. "I guess Eric isn't such a sadistic guide, after all."

"He certainly is very good-looking," Di sighed.

"You would think so," said Mart jealously. Pointing to his short blond hair, he muttered to Brian and Jim, "Maybe I should grow wild curls myself. They seem to drive the ladies mad."

"Don't you dare!" cried Di. "We like you just the way you are. You're a real individual, Mart."

"Good-bye, wild curls—hello, Di," Mart said happily. "Anyway, curls would cause too much of a resemblance to my beloved sibling Beatrix, which would be a catastrophe. Speaking of which"—he turned to Trixie—"I saw you eyeing Eric before the ski lesson, and you had that schoolgirl shamus look on your face. What's up?"

"I don't know, dear twin," answered Trixie, tossing her own sandy curls. "I'd ask your advice if you were good for anything but getting haircuts. Eric seems awfully nice, but there's just something about him. . . ."

"I thought it was sweet, the way he was worrying about his mother just because she got called away on business and didn't have time to phone him personally," said Honey, brushing the snow off her pants.

Trixie didn't say anything more as they set off along the small knolls on the top of the mountain ridge. As she slid into the easy rhythm of skiing, she was too fascinated with exploring this hidden trail to think any more about Eric. She was content to enjoy being part of the beauty and stillness of nature. She felt that she fully understood what cross-country skiing was all about.

The others seemed to share her feeling, and they skied along in silence for quite some time, as though the sound of their voices might knock the snow from off the branches.

Eventually Honey remarked, "I feel just like Lewis or Clark, setting off to chart lands far away from civilization. It's all so gorgeous and quiet. It's as though we're the only people in the world."

"It certainly seems that way," agreed Trixie, "but look way over on the side of that hill across the gully." She pointed with her ski pole. "There's a little house hidden in the trees."

The group halted in their tracks. "I see it," said Brian. "It's probably a way station or survival cabin, or maybe even a ski patrol hut."

"I doubt it," said Jim. "There wouldn't be enough people traveling through here to make use of those things. It could be a mountain man's abandoned cabin."

"You guys have no imagination," Mart said mischievously. "It's obviously an old prospector's hideaway. It's full of gold just *waiting* for Trixie to come along and rediscover it and make us all rich."

Trixie playfully grabbed a handful of snow and tossed it at Mart. Then she was silent for a few minutes. Finally she announced, "You know, that cabin *would* be a good hiding place so far back in the woods. I think we ought to go over and explore it."

"I've created a monster," Mart groaned.

"Don't be ridiculous, Trixie," Brian chided her.

"Besides, it must be almost time we head back for the lodge," Honey said reasonably. "We want to be out of the woods before it gets dark."

"And Vermont is farther north than Sleepyside, so it will get dark sooner," Jim reminded her.

"Oh, I suppose you're right," said Trixie, disappointed. "But it seems like every time I want to explore something mysterious, all of you vote me down. Doesn't being the Bob-White president count for anything?" she asked plaintively.

"Copresident," Jim corrected her. "And no, it doesn't count for anything, at least in this instance. Besides, there's nothing mysterious about an old cabin in the woods. They're all over the countryside."

Feeling very frustrated, Trixie lifted her ski to lead the way back down the trail. Too late she discovered she'd been standing on that ski with her other ski. Losing her balance, she plunged headlong into a snow-drift.

She heard some smothered chortling above her after Mart said something about a sitzmark, and she decided not to move, uncomfortable as she was. *Maybe they will think I'm dead and go away,* she thought, too upset to be rational.

But they didn't. Instead, Brian reached down and pulled her out. "You okay, Trix?" he asked, trying to hide the fact that he was weak from laughter.

"No, Brian Belden, I am not okay," Trixie said furiously. "I'm suffering from all of your superiority complexes, which, I might add, are totally erroneous, since you are not the least bit superior. But I'll tell you this, if there's anything funny going on in that cabin, I'll find out!" And with that, off she skied toward the lodge.

"Oh, Trixie," said Brian, starting to follow her.

Honey grabbed his arm. "Let her go. She's had her feelings hurt."

"It's no fun falling, either. I should know," added Di, rubbing her sore hip. "I thought I'd never get the hang of herringboning."

"Don't worry about her, Brian. Trixie knows there's no mystery in that cabin just as much as the rest of us do," said Honey, not particularly convincingly.

Trixie had skied off most of her resentment toward the others by the time they all got back to the lodge. At the base of the chair lift, they met Eric.

"What's the verdict?" he asked. "How do you like our little mountain?"

"It's just beautiful," said Honey enthusiastically.

"It's stupendous," agreed Jim. "And so is cross-country skiing!"

"Words fail me," Mart put in. "Except the words I had for you when we were climbing that crest."

"I told you that wouldn't be easy," Eric said. "Did you take one of the trails to the right, as I suggested?"

"We didn't know if you meant right facing the lodge or right facing the valley," Di answered.

"I meant right facing the valley."

"In that case, we went left," Trixie told him. "We saw something very interesting, too—an old cabin."

"You didn't go there, did you?" Eric demanded.

He seems nervous, thought Trixie.

"Why, no," said Honey. "Is there something special about it that we should go see?"

"Don't bother," he replied. "I was there yesterday. It's a dusty old cabin. It's abandoned now and rotted through. I'd stay away from there if I were you. It's dangerous."

That's funny, Trixie thought to herself. *I could have sworn I saw smoke coming out of the chimney.* She didn't say anything to the others, realizing that they weren't ready yet to hear her suspicions. But she decided to explore that cabin the very next chance she could get.

All squabbles forgotten, the Bob-Whites burst into their suite to find Miss Trask reading a book on the couch in front of the fire. "How was your afternoon?" she asked, slipping in her bookmark.

"Oh, we had the most marvelous time, Miss Trask," Honey began. "We'll tell you all about it. But first, may I have my watch? I was so worried when I couldn't find it this morning, and then Jim remembered that you must have taken it to hold on to for safekeeping."

"What do you mean, Honey? What watch?" Miss Trask inquired calmly.

"You don't have my grandmother's gold watch?"

Miss Trask shook her head. "No. What happened?"

Honey's eyes filled with tears. "It's gone! We'll never find it now!" She tore into the bedroom and threw herself down on the bottom bunk, sobbing.

Trixie followed her, even though she wasn't sure what to do or say. Honey was the one who was good in situations like this. From the bedroom, she could hear Di and the boys explaining everything to Miss Trask. Trixie sat down on the bunk next to Honey and put her arm around her friend.

"Honey, we'll find that watch," she said firmly. "We'll go through the entire suite again. We'll talk to Pat and Katie. We won't leave Mead's Mountain until we find out what happened to it!"

"Oh, Trixie, I wish we'd never come to this place," Honey wailed.

"I didn't want to tell you this until we'd talked to Miss Trask," Trixie said hesitantly, "but—Honey, I think your watch may have been stolen."

"Stolen?" Honey sat up.

"Remember how our front door was unlocked when we came back from swimming, but the patio door to the pool was mysteriously locked? Someone could have seen us swimming, come into the suite, locked the patio door so we wouldn't disturb him, and taken your watch."

"Why wouldn't he have taken other things, too?" Honey asked logically. "And who would do something like that, anyway?"

"Don't you remember running into Eric right near our front door?" asked Trixie.

"He was looking for Rosie," said Honey.

"Oh, Honey," said Trixie impatiently, "can't you see? Wanda's quarters disappeared the day Eric arrived. Your watch was discovered missing right after we saw Eric outside of our room."

"It is kind of suspicious, isn't it?" said Honey.

"He must have just come into the room when we were getting out of the pool," Trixie continued. "When we started banging on the door, he grabbed the first thing he saw—your watch—and quickly left. That's when we met him in the hall."

"You're probably right," sighed Honey. "But that doesn't help me get my watch back."

"We'll have to report it missing to the police and

Pat," Trixie decided. "Then we'll have to keep a very close eye on ol' Eric. Don't worry, Honey. I just know you'll get your watch back before we have to leave Mead's Mountain."

"Trixie, one other thing," Honey faltered. "You don't suppose our friendly neighborhood ghost took my watch, do you?"

Trixie was sure that the "ghost" was tied in somehow with this, but she was trying to calm Honey down, not upset her more. "I don't think so," she said. "Stealing doesn't seem like a very 'ghostly' thing to do."

"I wouldn't know," Honey said, shivering. "I've never met a ghost before, real or not. And you know what? I don't think I want to start making their acquaintance now!"

"I don't think you'll have to," Trixie said, hugging her friend. "I'm sure Eric took your watch. Right now let's worry about dinner. Who can go sleuthing on an empty stomach for valuable family heirlooms?"

Honey giggled. "Now you're beginning to sound like Mart!"

Snowfield Danger • 7

THE FOLLOWING MORNING dawned bright and beautiful again, but the Bob-Whites, exhausted from their first day on the mountain, decided to sleep in late.

At nine, Miss Trask awoke the girls to tell them that a policeman had come to get a full report on the missing watch. Trixie decided not to tell him anything about seeing Eric around their room. She could prove nothing, and she had a feeling that if she just bided her time, Eric would prove himself the thief without any help from her.

After the policeman left, Trixie and Honey called the only pawnshop in Groverville to see if the watch had been pawned. The pawnbroker was a pleasant, talkative man who called himself Pawnbroker Joe.

He asked all about the watch and all about the girls. Although he hadn't seen the watch, he was very sympathetic about Honey's loss, and he promised to let them know if he heard anything about it.

Miss Trask joined the Bob-Whites for their swim that morning and enjoyed it as much as they did. Afterward, they all got dressed for breakfast. Honey's blue and brown outfit and Di's purple ensemble both had come from an exclusive ski shop, but Trixie felt that their outfits weren't any more becoming than her own. The cream and powder blue sweater Moms had knit her for Christmas went perfectly with the blue ski pants that Brian and Mart had given her. You couldn't buy a sweater as special as Moms could make. Trixie could tell by the approving looks she received that she looked nice.

Once they got to the restaurant, the Bob-Whites decided to have a big breakfast and no lunch, since the morning was nearly gone already. During the course of conversation, it developed that not one of them wanted to attempt the steep climb above the chair lift they had experienced the day before.

"Why don't we ski through the woods just above the bunny tow?" suggested Brian. "It's easily accessible, and we can check out good places for picnicking and fishing. I'll bet Mr. Wheeler would appreciate that information."

Following up on Brian's suggestion, the group found plenty of material for their notebooks. That part of the woods was full of all kinds of fascinating foliage.

"Dad really ought to organize a nature hike through

this area," Jim said. "He could have signs labeling each of the different types of trees, flowers, and shrubs."

"The signs could tell a little bit about each, too," Trixie offered. "Like that tree—isn't it a sugar maple?"

Jim nodded. "Vermont is famous for maple syrup. A sign near that tree might tell all about sapping time and making maple sugar and syrup."

"When I was in one of those stuffy boarding schools," said Honey a bit sadly, "I read a book all about some kids gathering sap. I remember wanting to join them so badly."

"How did they do it, Honey?" asked Di.

"Well, it sounded pretty easy," Honey recalled. "They pushed a pipelike thing called a spile into the tree, and the sap dripped out into a bucket hanging from the tree. Then they gathered up the sap and boiled it down into syrup and maple sugar. They kept the pots covered with screens so dirt and stuff wouldn't get in. I remember that part because the youngest boy, who was a little older than Bobby, had to take one of the horses back to the house to get the screens. The boy was really proud to be able to do that alone."

"Oh, that sounds like fun!" exclaimed Di. "Wouldn't our parents be surprised if we brought home some maple syrup we had made ourselves?"

"Surprised? They'd probably award us the Pulitzer prize for achieving the impossible," commented Mart. "Sorry, Di, but the sap doesn't start running until mid-February at the earliest. It's the rise and fall in temperature that makes the sap start flowing. But, you know, we could tell Mr. Wheeler that maple sapping parties here would be a great activity in the early spring."

More possibilities for the nature hike were spotted as the Bob-Whites skied on through the woods, laughing and joking. At one point, Jim, who was in the lead, stopped abruptly.

"Dead end," he called back. "We've come to a stream. Looks good for fishing, but it's the end of the road as far as skiing is concerned."

"It is too wide to cross," agreed Honey, joining him at the edge of the rocky creek. "Why don't we follow it to see where it goes?"

Off they skied, only to be stopped again by Jim in a few hundred yards. This time he didn't say a word, just held up his hand. The others, catching up to him, sensed the need to be quiet, but gave him quizzical looks.

Then they followed his gaze and saw two deer, magnificent graceful creatures, drinking from the opposite side of the creek. Every line of their bodies had a smooth purposefulness to it. One doe lifted her head and, looking directly at Trixie, stood as motionless as a piece of sculpture.

"They know we're here!" gasped Trixie.

"Yes, but I don't think they'll be afraid of us as long as we don't make any sudden moves," Jim whispered back.

"I'm beginning to feel guilty about that roast venison we had at your house," Di said softly.

Honey nodded, her eyes shining. "Come on. Let's go

on and leave these deer in peace."

A little farther up the stream, Jim noticed a large tree that had fallen across, making a natural bridge. It was hard to tell how safe it was.

"I'm sure it's rotted through, Jim," Honey insisted. "And I refuse to set one foot on it."

"But its roots look perfectly healthy. I'll go across very slowly. If it holds my weight, it will hold us all."

"Jim, please," Honey wailed.

Jim took off his skis. "Brian, will you hold my hand as I start out? Don't worry, Honey."

Gingerly he tested each step with his ski pole before advancing. Trixie could see that he was being very cautious, but she held her breath just the same till he reached the other side.

"Solid as can be," he called encouragingly.

One by one, the others followed him. Di and Honey hung back uncertainly until Trixie, acting braver than she felt, took her skis off and walked directly across the large log.

"Just take a deep breath and go, but don't look down," she advised the others.

Mart poked her with his ski pole. " 'Tis useless to advertise your heroism—excuse me, heroine-ism—in my hearing, sis. I saw you go green around the gills when *you* looked down."

Unable to think of a retort, Trixie contented herself for the time being with poking him right back.

On this side of the stream, the terrain was more rugged, which suited Trixie just fine. Ready for a faster pace, she seized her first opportunity for it when they reached a long, steep, curving downhill grade. She let those in front of her get far ahead. She didn't want any slowpokes in her way when she took this hill by storm. Just to be on the safe side, she hollered the skier's warning of "Track!" as she began gaining speed down the hill. This was fun—almost like flying without a plane!

At about the same time she remembered Eric's caution about avoiding obstacles long before coming to them, Trixie began to suspect that she was losing control. She could see a curve up ahead, and she crouched farther down on her skis, putting her weight on her right foot. One ski made the turn, but the other insisted on going straight ahead. The next thing she knew, Trixie found herself wound around a clump of bushes, half on the path, half in the brush.

Her glorious flight had ended with a crash landing. She didn't seem to be hurt, only stunned. But she was definitely caught in the bushes.

I've got to get up, she thought. *Brian's still behind me, and I'm blocking the path.* After one last desperate attempt to pull herself off the path, she covered her head with her arms.

She should have known that Brian, sensible as ever, would be taking the hill slower than she'd tried to take it. "Trixie!" she heard him yell. Peeking upward, she saw him coming straight at her. He managed to avoid her, but he couldn't stop in time to avoid toppling into the snowdrift on the other side of the path.

Instantly he scrambled to his feet and rushed to her side. "Trix, you okay?"

"Brian, I feel fine, but I just can't move."

Brian forgot his doctor-to-be manners and burst out laughing. "That's because you're a human pretzel. I don't think I've ever seen anyone so wound up!"

Trixie glared at him. "Don't just laugh—unwind me."

By the time Trixie and Brian caught up, the others were out of the woods, waiting impatiently at the edge of a large snowfield.

"Hey, where have you two been?" scolded Honey. "You're holding us up from crossing no-man's-land."

"Obstacle on the trail," said Brian, pointing to Trixie.

"Has our sister been schussbooming again?" Mart inquired.

"I don't know what that is," Trixie said stormily. "I was merely knocked over by some bushes."

"You're a schussboomer, *ipso facto,*" Mart teased. "Case dismissed."

Trixie sighed noisily. Mart was beginning to get on her nerves.

Acting as peacemaker, Di spoke up. "We dubbed this no-man's-land because it looks as though no one has ever crossed the field before."

Trixie saw what Di meant. There was an overhanging cliff at one end of the smooth, glassy snowfield, and a winding river marked the boundary on the opposite side. On the other two sides were woods.

"Hey, look!" Trixie exclaimed. "There's another skier!" She pointed to the other side of the snowfield. Someone had just come out of the woods and was starting across the broad expanse toward them.

"Hello!" Honey called, waving her arms over her

head. The skier stopped, seemed to look at them, and quickly disappeared back into the woods.

"Well, he certainly isn't very friendly," said Honey. "And everyone else at Mead's Mountain has been so nice."

"Except our ghost," Di reminded her.

"He's probably just another tourist like us," Jim said. "Did you get a load of his ski mask? It was green and red—really grotesque."

"Who would wear a ski mask on such a warm day?" Trixie asked idly.

"Someone who doesn't want to get sunburned," retorted Brian. "If you would look in a mirror once in a while, Trixie, you'd see for yourself what a red-nosed reindeer *you* are. Just like the rest of you poor fair-skinned blonds and redheads." He and Di had tanned beautifully the previous day.

"Well, at least we match the season," Honey told him.

"That skier shot our no-man's-land theory all to pieces, didn't he?" said Jim.

"Why don't we follow him and see where he's going?" suggested Trixie.

"Trixie, he obviously didn't want to socialize," Brian sighed. "Come on! Let's have a race to the other side instead!"

They all tore after him, yelling and laughing. Not far off in the distance, Trixie heard the roar of thunder. *Who would have thought we could have a thunderstorm on such a beautiful day?* she mused, struggling to overtake Brian. *It seems too cold to rain.*

She looked over at Jim beside her and saw his face turn stark white. That's when she knew it wasn't thunder she heard.

"Avalanche!" Jim screamed over the growing roar. "Get out of here!"

Trixie skied harder than she ever had before. She couldn't tell anymore if the booming she heard was the rumble of the avalanche or the pounding of her own heart.

Just when she was sure she was going to faint, she felt the vibrations of the avalanche passing behind her. She was safe!

Then she heard a new sound—one as terrifying as the avalanche roar itself. Whirling around to find the source of those shrill cries, Trixie saw her brother Mart rolling down the hill and then disappearing underneath what looked like tons of snow.

Clues and Conversations • 8

MART! MART!" Trixie shrieked. "Oh, Mart's been caught in the avalanche, everyone!" Without waiting for a response, she started skiing back across the snowfield, calling out Mart's name all the time she was battling through mounds of snow.

"Trixie, wait!" Jim called.

Brian took off after Trixie. "What do you mean, wait?" he asked angrily. "That's our brother!"

Trixie, defeated by the uneven terrain, lost control of her skis and fell face first into the snow. She could feel her hot tears mixing with the icy snow.

As Brian was helping her to her feet, Jim caught up with them. "Will you two listen to me?" he pleaded. "Mart is in a lot of trouble, but we're all going to be in trouble if we ski around like chickens with our heads cut off. You both know that panic in a situation like this is very dangerous, so will you just simmer down for a minute?"

Trixie couldn't believe that Jim could be so callous. "Jim, *I* am going to find Mart," she fumed, "even if *you* don't seem to care what happened to him."

Honey and Di had joined them, and Honey took Trixie's arm. "See the rest of that snow?" she asked, pointing to the cliff above them. "That could go any minute, Trixie. We'd all be caught. Who'd help Mart then?"

Trixie sank back weakly. "You're right, you guys. I'm not thinking straight."

"It's just that it's Mart under all that snow," said Brian somberly. "What do we do now?"

"Di, you keep an eye on the cliff for any movement at all," Jim decided. "In case of trouble, everyone head for the woods." As he was talking, Jim took a length of rope out of his knapsack and tied it around his waist. He instructed each of them to do the same. "If we get caught in another avalanche, pretend to swim in the snow. That will help you stay on the surface, but if you don't, the rope will float up and you'll be easier to find. It was stupid not to do this before we crossed this field. Heavy snowfall the other night, sun the last couple of days, the overhanging snow, and no trees—why didn't we recognize this as a potential slide area?" In disgust, he pulled tight on the knot in his rope. "And I like to think of myself as a woodsman."

"No, it's all my fault," said Brian. "I suggested the race."

"Don't be silly!" Honey cried. "It's nobody's fault. Let's concentrate on saving Mart instead of blaming ourselves."

Jim turned to Trixie. "Where did you last see him?"

"About ten yards from here. He came so close to outskiing the avalanche. He was right on the edge of it." Trixie led the others to the place where she thought she had seen Mart disappear.

Not too far from there, Di noticed something dark sticking out of the snow. She grabbed Brian's arm and pointed excitedly. "Look, look, what's that?"

Brian skied over and picked up the object. He turned it over in his hand and said slowly, "It's a piece of Mart's ski."

Trixie moaned.

"Come on, let's put our skis in the woods first," Jim urged. Everyone obeyed, and Jim continued, "Let's start at the bottom of the slide area. Each person stand about two feet from the next person. Turn one ski pole upside down and stick it into the snow every foot as we walk up the hill. If you feel any resistance—any at all—yell. But not too loudly. Even the vibrations of our voices could start another avalanche."

As they started up the hill, Trixie tried to banish from her mind the picture of Mart lying buried under all the snow, but it was an impossible task. "How long do we have, Jim?" she asked tensely.

"If we can't find him in an hour, we'll have to send for help." That was all Jim would say.

What he means is, if we don't find him in an hour, it may be too late, Trixie cried silently.

No one said anything for a long time. They were too intent on poking their poles into the snow as far as they could. Finally, Trixie's prayers seemed to be answered: Her ski pole went down a few feet and would go no farther.

"Jim! Brian! Everyone! My pole hit something!"

They all raced over to her and started digging in the snow with their hands. When they uncovered a large flat-topped boulder, Trixie stared at it for a moment, refusing to believe that Mart was still missing. Then, without a word, she got up and started poking her pole into the snow again.

Minutes later, Brian gave a jubilant cry. Again Trixie joined in the digging, but this time she didn't get excited. Brian had probably found another boulder . . . or Mart smashed against a boulder. Then she scraped away just enough of the powdery white to reveal some of the green fuzz of Mart's sweater, and her troubled tears became tears of joy. He was alive!

Working quickly and carefully, they dug him out of his snowy prison and got him back into the woods where they had left their skis. He appeared to be all right, but for what seemed like ages he just sat against a tree, taking deep breaths and blinking the snow out of his eyes. While he recovered, Brian checked for broken bones and took his pulse, and Jim brewed him a cup of tea over the Sterno fuel from his survival kit.

After a few sips of tea, Mart was finally able to speak. "I can't believe I'm here! When I realized

I wasn't going to make it, I kept my arms around my face so I'd have some breathing room. After I was good and buried, I tried to dig my way out, but by then I wasn't sure which way was up. You can't imagine what it's like to be buried alive. I thought you guys would never find me! I—I even said if I could just get out of there, I'd never tease Trixie again!"

"Does anybody have a tape recorder?" Trixie asked. She tried her best to sound sarcastic, but a beaming grin gave her away.

"Well, at least I can make some suggestions to Mr. Wheeler about avalanche control," said Mart, smiling weakly as he reached into his pocket for his rather smashed notebook.

"Jeepers, Mart, how cool, calm, and collected can you be?" cried Honey. "You just about got yourself killed and already you're cracking jokes!"

"I'm collected enough to be glad my skis are broken," he replied. "I don't think I want to do any more skiing today."

"Really?" teased Di. "And I thought you'd be game for a race to go over and explore those caves."

"What caves?" Trixie queried.

"Didn't you see those caves up on the hill on the other side of the river?" Di asked. "I guess you can't see them from here, but I noticed them as we were crossing the avalanche area. Maybe after Mart feels better, we could come back to explore them."

"They're probably just holes in the rocks, Di—not interesting enough to explore," Jim told her. "These mountains were formed by an uplift of land from pressure out in the ocean. There's no elaborate underground river system."

"Let's quit gabbing and get Mart back to the lodge," Brian recommended. "Getting buried in an avalanche is not exactly what the doctor ordered. He's going to need some rest."

"And some warm food," Mart quickly prescribed for himself.

"Gleeps, he's thinking of food already," said Trixie with relief. "He *must* be all right!"

Mart seemed to have gained all his strength back by the time they reached the lodge. When Katie heard about Mart's misfortune, she arranged for a special dinner featuring his favorite food, hamburgers.

At dinner, Bert Mitchell and Jack Caridiff stopped by the Bob-Whites' table to listen to their tales of woe about the avalanche and Honey's missing watch.

Jack looked apprehensive. "It's the ghost of Thomas Mead, I tell you," he said.

Everyone, except Mart, stopped chewing their hamburgers. Trixie narrowed her eyes, watching Jack closely to see if he really believed what he was saying. He seemed very sincere.

"I'm sure you're pulling our leg," Honey said politely but skeptically.

"Jack's just a mite superstitious," Bert started to explain.

Jack shook his head. "Everyone's taking this whole business of the ghost too lightly," he insisted. "If this lodge is haunted, not one of us is safe."

"Now, Mr. Caridiff," said Miss Trask in her no-

nonsense way, "I'm sure that the ghost of Thomas Mead is just folklore the people of this area like to keep alive. Just like our Hudson River ghosts. Those stories get better with each generation."

"Right," said Mart, reaching for dessert. "Haven't you heard of the legend of Sleepy Hollow?"

"The headless horseman," recalled Jack, "who can still be seen riding through the woods on stormy nights."

"Just like you saw the ghost of Mead's Mountain our first night here, Trixie," Brian teased.

Trixie made a face at him and finished up her meal. She still believed that what she had seen had been real, not just her imagination's reaction to folklore.

Bert stood up. "I've got a good magazine waiting for me," he said. "If you're through with the ghost stories, Jack, are you coming, too?"

"I think I'll stay and have another cup of tea," Jack decided. "How about you, Miss Trask? May I bring you a refill?"

"That would be nice," she said, handing him her cup.

Brian, Di, Jim, and Mart decided to head back to the suite for some rest. Before exiting, Mart offered Trixie his arm and inquired formally, "Coming, Ms. Belden?"

"Thank you for your concern," she replied sweetly. "I think I'll just sit here and digest my dinner for a while."

After he had gone, Honey leaned over and whispered, "What gives, Trixie?"

"I've been *waiting* for him to leave," Trixie giggled. "I want another piece of that lemon meringue pie, and I don't want to hear all of his you'd-better-watch-your-waistline jokes."

Honey laughed. "I'll join you," she said enthusiastically. "We can afford it with all the extra exercise we're getting."

Just as the girls were savoring their first bites of the pie, all of the lights in the entire restaurant began to dim . . . slowly . . . slowly. Their forks in midair, Trixie and Honey stared at each other, wide-eyed. Then the lights went off completely, and they couldn't see a thing. Before either of them could say a word, the lights flashed on again! Just as suddenly, they were off.

On and off the lights flickered several times, until they went out for good, leaving Trixie, Honey, Miss Trask, and Jack sitting in total darkness.

Jack was the first to say anything. "It's the ghost! He heard us talking and didn't like it!"

Miss Trask, always cool in any kind of crisis, said briskly, "I'm sure it's a power failure. Electrical equipment is not always stable in remote areas."

"I wish we had our survival kits," said Trixie. "A flashlight would sure be— Oh, here comes Wanda with some candles." Thanking Wanda, she added, "I guess you're prepared for any emergency around here."

Jack lit his candle and stood up to leave. "Are you all ready to go now?" he asked them.

"We're not quite done with our pie," said Trixie.

"But if you're ready, Miss Trask, perhaps Jack would see you back to the suite."

"My pleasure," said Jack.

"You won't be long, will you, girls?" asked Miss Trask before she left.

"No," promised Trixie. "But I do feel like a little fresh air. I thought we might walk around the outside of the building on our way back to the room."

"Don't get too cold," Miss Trask cautioned. "You've only got on your sweaters."

"I'll make sure she doesn't get too much fresh air, Miss Trask," said Honey.

As soon as Jack and Miss Trask had gone, Trixie pushed away her pie and hurried Honey outside. Before they could get far, Honey grabbed Trixie's arm. "Okay, Trixie, I know you well enough to know you didn't have a sudden urge for fresh air. What's going on?"

"All the electricity to the lodge must be controlled by a breaker switch," Trixie told her. "Breaker switches are usually located on the outside of buildings."

"Trixie, you're so smart," her friend said admiringly. "But what does this have to do with us?"

"Well, wouldn't it be easy for a 'ghost' to cause a power outage by throwing a switch? If we can find the breaker switch, maybe we can find some clues."

"How are we going to find the breaker switch?" Honey objected. "This candle isn't giving off very much light."

"I wish we could go back to the suite for a flashlight," fretted Trixie. "But if we did, Miss Trask would never let us come back outside again."

"You're right about that," said a voice behind the two girls.

They both jumped, and Trixie whirled around. "Oh, Mart," she gasped, "don't you know any better than to sneak up on people? Especially when the lights are all out? And there's talk of a ghost?"

"Not only did I not buy your story about 'digesting dinner for a while,'" retorted her brother, "but I don't think Miss Trask bought your fabrication about needing fresh air after a full day on the slopes. That's probably why she asked me to bring you these flashlights."

Trixie gave him a grateful smile.

The three of them had no trouble finding the breaker box on the west side of the main building. The switch had definitely been turned off, Trixie noticed, immediately using her flashlight to look for footprints. The walkway around the lodge was blurred with indistinguishable footprints, and none of them veered over to the breaker switch. However, anyone could have reached the breaker switch from the path.

Trixie kicked at the snow in disappointment. "No clues here."

"I wouldn't be too sure," said Mart, pointing his flashlight.

Trixie's eyes followed the beam. There, on top of the breaker box, was a neatly folded piece of paper. On the outside, written in red block letters, was her name.

She grabbed it and nervously unfolded it. Honey

and Mart crowded close to her and directed their lights toward the paper, illuminating its message:

YOUR LIFE IS IN DANGER
T.L.M.

Trixie quickly crumpled the note up.

"Oh, Trixie," Honey wailed.

"This is carrying a practical joke a little too far," Mart burst out. "Besides, if your life's 'in danger,' what about mine? *I* was the one caught in the avalanche today!"

"Yipes, Mart," said Trixie, startled, "you don't think that—that this note is connected with the avalanche, do you?"

"Of course not. I'm sure that this note is from the same joker who broke into our room the first night. And I don't think we should mention this to Miss Trask, in case she takes it too seriously and gets worried unnecessarily. This note is simply a prank," Mart decided. "My inundation with snow was just an unfortunate accident of nature."

Just then they heard Pat coming around the corner, saying, "I thought it might be the generator. It seems to go out regularly. I didn't even think about the switch box, Eric."

"Come on," Trixie whispered, "let's get out of here before we have to explain this note to Pat and Eric."

Leaving Pat and Eric to take care of getting the lights back on, they raced back to their suite, where the others were just putting out the fire and getting ready for bed. Trixie was only too glad to go right to bed and avoid talking with anyone.

She was exhausted, but even after she could hear Di and Honey's even breathing, she could not seem to will herself to sleep. The ghostly figure she had seen, Eric, the missing watch and quarters, the mess their room had been, the avalanche, the cabin in the woods, and the note addressed to her—all churned through her mind, making sleep impossible.

She became worried that her tossing and turning would wake up Di and Honey, so she slid out of bed, put on her bathrobe, and stepped out onto the balcony as quietly as she could.

By the light of the moon and its reflection on the snow, Trixie could see the outline of the mountains against the sky. She took deep breaths of the cleansing mountain air.

Gradually she became aware of voices and figures somewhere out in the woods around the lodge. The first voice she recognized immediately as Eric's.

"I just wish you had told me sooner, that's all," he was saying.

"Hush, keep your voice down. Someone might hear," replied a voice Trixie had never heard before.

"I want to help. I want to do anything I can," Eric was pleading.

"Well, the money's good, no need to worry about that. If you want to search the woods, you can."

"Of course I want to!" Eric answered, his voice raised a little.

"Hush!"

"Okay, okay!"

"Just remember—stay away from the police," the stranger warned. Then he added, "I'll let you know how things are going."

Straining her eyes, Trixie saw one of the figures move out of the clump of woods and disappear around the corner of the lodge. She couldn't make out what happened to the second figure.

She'd been too intent on catching what was said to realize she'd been eavesdropping. Now that the conversation was over, she felt a twinge of guilt. *Still,* she thought excitedly, *I'm onto something. And whatever it is, is causing someone to try to scare us away from the lodge. But what does it all mean?*

Long after Trixie returned to bed, the puzzling words of the two moonlit figures tumbled in her brain, until finally she fell into a troubled sleep.

Mr. Moonshine • 9

A DISTURBING DREAM jolted Trixie awake the next morning, and she was the first one up. Gently she nudged Honey awake and beckoned her into the living room. The cloudy, damp day prompted them to get a fire going, and soon they were huddling in front of the warmth, Trixie relating the conversation she'd overheard to Honey.

"Trixie, how strange!" Honey bubbled over. "You're right—something's going on. But what?"

"I've been up half the night, and I still don't have any idea. But you know what? I think Eric's our ghost."

"Someone could have told him we're detectives," Honey reasoned. "He could be afraid we'll discover what he's really doing, so he's trying to scare us away."

"Or maybe he's playing these practical jokes to keep us occupied chasing a ghost, while he goes merrily on his way stealing watches and quarters and whatever else he can get," Trixie conjectured.

"You've got it, Trixie! Eric and the guy he was talking with are part of a burglary ring!"

" 'The money's good' could mean that they'll make a lot of money doing it," said Trixie with growing confidence. But what about the 'search the woods' part?"

"Jeepers, I don't have any idea. That part's really mystifying."

"Listen," urged Trixie, "let's go back and explore that cabin we saw in the woods. I didn't mention this before, but I'm pretty sure I saw smoke coming out the chimney, and, you know, even Mart said something about the cabin's being a perfect hiding place."

"But Eric said it was rotten and abandoned," Honey objected.

"That's exactly why I want to explore it! After what I heard last night, I'm not going to trust what Eric says for a minute. Come on, let's wake up the others. I want to get to that cabin as soon as possible."

Much to their surprise and delight, the Bob-Whites found it easier to make the climb through the woods above the chair lift that morning. They showed better control of their skis, and their muscles were getting accustomed to the rigors of mountain sports. The day was turning out to be another perfect sunny one.

Trixie waited until they were all resting at the top

of the ridge before announcing her intention to go back to the cabin.

"No way," said Brian sternly. "Mr. Wheeler hired us to explore all the area around here, not to try to solve some mystery."

"Explore the area—that's just what I want to do, Brian. Only I want to explore over there," said Trixie, pointing down the hidden trail. Although she felt she just *had* to investigate that cabin, she knew Brian was right about their responsibility to Mr. Wheeler. They did have a job to do, and they'd given their word to Mr. Wheeler that they would do a good one, too.

Tactful Honey came up with a solution. "Why don't we split up, and Trixie and I go back to the cabin, while the rest of you explore in another direction?" she suggested. "We have to make the best use of our week here, and we really should check out any possibility of emergency shelter for lost skiers."

"You have a point," Jim conceded. "And I know Trixie will make us miserable until she gets back to that cabin. I'll go with you so you don't get lost or something."

"Don't bother," said Trixie defiantly. "We can take care of ourselves. We won't get lost, but if, by some remote chance, we do, we have our survival kits and know how to use them. Come on, Honey."

As they skied off down the hidden trail, Honey said wistfully, "I wouldn't have minded if Jim had come along, Trixie. He's been a big help to us more than once."

"Oh, I know," answered Trixie, biting her lip. "I've

just got to learn to control my temper."

"Do you think there's any easier way to get to that cabin besides climbing up that steep gully?" asked Honey, without much hope.

"I've been thinking about that," replied Trixie. "That gully looked to me like it's probably just a trench with a beginning and an end. I remember seeing a smaller path that forked off to the right down the trail a bit. Maybe it leads to the other side of that trench and to the cabin."

Sure enough, before too long they caught sight of the cabin on their side of the gully. They skied for a while until they reached a large pine tree. Triumphantly, Trixie pointed out the smoke wisping out of the chimney. She could even see ski tracks leading to the door of the old structure.

"Now what?" asked Honey, starting to tremble a bit. "Someone is obviously there. Maybe someone is even living there!"

"Now we just go knock on the door," decided Trixie, showing far more courage than she felt. She skied up to the front door and rapped boldly on it before Honey could protest.

The door was thrown open by a spry old man with a shock of long white hair. A stern frown lined his face, and his red bulky knit sweater made his cold blue eyes seem even colder. His obvious displeasure made Trixie uneasy.

"Who are you," he demanded, towering over her, "and what are you doing here?"

Trixie gulped. Not until that very moment did it

dawn on her that she'd prepared absolutely nothing to say. She had acted again without thinking things through.

Nervous though she was, Honey managed to come to the rescue. "I—I'm Honey Wheeler, and this is Trixie Belden," she stammered, "and we're out skiing, and, well, we wondered if we might have a drink of water."

This request seemed to enrage the old man even more than their presence did. He grabbed a ski pole and brandished it at the girls.

"This is private property," he hissed, "and I don't ever—I mean ever—want to see you here again. Now, beat it!" The door slammed in their faces.

Trixie and Honey were too stunned to do anything but obey. After herringboning as rapidly as they could back up the gully, they skied until they were well out of sight of the cabin before stopping under a tree to rest.

"Was I glad when you asked for a drink!" exclaimed Trixie gratefully. "I couldn't think of a thing to say, except to ask him who *he* was and what *he* was doing there."

Honey had to giggle. "I don't think that would have gone over very well, Trixie."

Trixie smiled sheepishly and got a small can of orange juice out of her knapsack. "Well, at least we've solved the mystery of the long-haired 'ghost' that people have seen. There really *is* an old man living in the mountains. So that's who I saw the first night on our way here. What a grouch!"

"That must be why Eric told us to stay away," Honey speculated. "He knew we'd disturb him and make him angry."

Trixie seized Honey's arm. "Gleeps, Honey! That's the voice! I'm sure of it!"

"Huh? What voice?"

"The one Eric was talking with last night!"

"Are you sure, Trixie? This seems like an odd place for someone to live who's in a burglary ring. So far from anywhere."

"I'm positive," said her friend, finishing up her juice quickly. "Something funny is going on in that cabin. Listen, if you lived in the mountains this far away from people, wouldn't it be because you loved the mountains?"

"I suppose so."

"Then—would *you* keep all the curtains shut on such a beautiful day?"

"You're kidding! They were shut?"

"They sure were, and did you notice that funny smell?"

"Yes, now that you mention it. What was it?" asked Honey.

Trixie frowned, her forehead wrinkled in thought. "It smelled just like the alcohol we used in biology."

"Alcohol! Trixie, do you suppose he's—oh, you know . . . someone who makes liquor illegally—a moonshiner, that's it! Maybe he has a still in there!"

"I'll bet they have quite a little business going here," Trixie crowed. "The money in it would be good; they'd want to stay away from the police; and the woods would be the perfect center of operations!"

"And they certainly wouldn't appreciate us skiing around investigating the area. Nor would they want it sold as a natural resort area," added Honey, helping to put more pieces of the puzzle together.

"Come on, Honey, let's go tell the others about our new friend, Mr. Moonshine!"

By the time they got back to the lodge, the sky had clouded up again, and they were starving. Racing over to the restaurant, they found the others already finishing their lunch.

"Hey, where have you two been for so long?" queried Mart, looking up from his soup. "We thought you'd be back before this. Miss Trask was worried."

"Oh, dear, I didn't want to worry anyone on this trip, least of all Miss Trask," said Trixie. "She's such a good sport about everything."

"We assured her that you two are regular woodsmen and can take care of yourselves," said Brian, scraping the bottom of his bowl.

Trixie threw him a grateful look, then said, "Come on, Honey, let's get some of that soup."

"Wait a minute, Trix," Jim broke in. "There's more. Miss Trask was jumpy after the avalanche yesterday, and she wants us all to ski together from now on."

Honey nodded. "Where is she? I guess we'd better tell her we're back."

"She's in reading to Rosie," Di said. "Katie was telling us how Rosie always pretends to go to sleep but gets up and causes all kinds of mischief instead. Miss Trask offered to try to read her to sleep."

"Rosie sounds like Bobby," remarked Trixie.

"Go ahead and get some lunch," Di said. "I'll go tell Miss Trask you're back."

"One more thing, Trixie," said Brian. "Mart told us about the note you got last night."

"We're not trying to scare you," added Jim, "but do us a favor and don't go anywhere alone. Okay?"

"You two are being silly," Trixie began. Then she noticed their frowns and gave in. "Okay, if it'll make you happy."

After Di returned, Trixie and Honey told the group about the conversation that Trixie had overheard and described their encounter with the old man.

"Now we're getting some answers," said Jim. "You know, I've never been fully convinced that anything more than a few practical jokes was going on. But it sure sounds like your Mr. Moonshine and Eric are up to something more serious if they're so worried about staying away from the police."

"I don't know about the making liquor part, though," said Brian. "It could be just for himself, for medicinal purposes. It's not very likely he'd haul it out to sell. It would weigh far too much to carry, and there are no roads out there."

"He could put it on sleds and haul it to the nearest road," Trixie insisted. "You should have smelled his cabin, Brian. The place just reeked of alcohol. Maybe Eric helps him."

"You know what?" Di put in. "Eric's been gone all day. First thing this morning, he asked Pat for the day off, and instead of going to town, he took off into the mountains on skis. He isn't back yet."

"He's searching the woods," breathed Trixie. "Just like he was talking about last night!"

"Searching for *what?*" Mart objected, getting ready to attack Trixie's reasoning. Before he could continue, Linda and Wanda came over to join them.

"Hey, did you know it's raining outside?" asked Wanda.

Mart glanced up from the conversation they'd all been so intent on and commented, "So it is. Well, what a vicissitudinous day!"

"No, Mart, it's just rain," argued Di.

Amid the laughter, Brian grumbled, "That's going to spoil skiing for the rest of the day."

"Probably," Wanda agreed. "Pat and Katie told us there won't be many people left here in another hour, so that we could have the evening off if we like. We were wondering if you might like to go into town for dinner. We could give you a small tour first, and then take you to one of our favorite restaurants."

Their invitation met with an enthusiastic acceptance from the Bob-Whites.

"What should we wear?" Di asked immediately.

"We're going to the Purple Turnip," said Linda. "Wear something casual. Pants are fine."

"Whew!" said Jim, pretending to wipe the sweat from his brow.

"The Purple Turnip—what kind of a place is that?" asked Mart.

"A vegetarian restaurant," answered Wanda.

"Oh, no!" Mart let out an exaggerated groan. "I'm

a growing boy, you know. I need food! That's capital M-E-A-T. Maybe we'd better eat here first."

"Don't worry, you'll get plenty to eat, Mart," chuckled Wanda. "I'll make you a deal—if you're still hungry after dinner, I, personally, will fix you a giant hamburger with all the trimmings."

"I can taste it now!" said Mart appreciatively.

"It's a nice family-run restaurant," Linda told them. "They have a folk singer, too. I think you'll like it a lot."

"Have you told them about Jenny yet?" Wanda asked her twin.

Linda turned to the Bob-Whites and explained shyly, "Jenny is our little sister. She's a beautiful, wonderful, and very special person. Physically Jenny is nine, but because of the brain damage she suffered at birth, she has the mentality of a four-year-old."

"A very bright four-year-old," Wanda added. "She looks at the world with such joy—we can't help being very proud of her."

"If you don't mind," Linda said, "we'd like to stop in and see her before dinner. We try to see her every time we get into town. She'd enjoy meeting you. She likes company."

"Oh, we'd love to meet her!" exclaimed Honey.

"We have a few chores to do before we leave," Wanda said. "So we'll meet you about four if that's okay."

When it came time for the girls to get dressed for the trip into town, Di chanted playfully, "Oh, what to wear, what to wear? I brought two nice after-ski outfits, and I just can't make up my mind."

"I'll decide for you," Trixie offered. "Wear the rosy pink sweater and matching plaid pants. You look stunning in bright colors. Honey, why don't you wear your dark gold sweater and pants? With your hair, you'll look like the traditional golden girl. As for me, I will just be my average old self," she finished, pretending to sigh heavily.

"Jeepers, Trixie, you're about as un-average as they come," Honey told her.

"Sure," teased Di. "Just because you get average marks in a few subjects at school doesn't mean you're an all-around average person."

Trixie aimed a pillow in Di's direction and began changing into her navy blue turtleneck sweater and blue plaid slacks. Then she had an interesting idea. "If Eric's back, why don't we ask the twins if we could invite him along?" she suggested. "He's probably lonely. Maybe he'd enjoy an evening out."

Honey snorted, and even Di laughed.

Trixie became indignant. "What's your problem? I just thought it was a nice idea."

"Oh, Trixie! Of course, it's a good idea," said Honey. "But isn't it possible that maybe—just maybe—you were thinking more about getting another clue than about keeping Eric from being lonely?"

"Well. . . ."

Honey looked in the mirror and brushed her hair. "If you two are ready, why don't you go ask Linda and Wanda if we could invite Eric? I'll check on the slowpoke boys."

After speaking with Linda and Wanda, Di and Trixie stopped at Eric's door. "Sure you wouldn't rather invite him, Di? He seems to like you."

"Moonshining thieves aren't my style," sniffed Di, giving Trixie a push. "This was your idea."

Trixie knocked on the door.

"Who is it and what do you want?" called Eric, sounding weary and irritated.

"It's Trixie Belden. Linda, Wanda, and all of us are going into town to visit Linda and Wanda's sister and then go out to dinner. We wondered if you wanted to join us."

She heard some scuffling in the room, and then the door opened. Eric was wearing an undershirt and jeans that were wet from skiing in the rain. His hair was messed up, and there were bags under his eyes. "You're going to dinner in town? In a restaurant?" he inquired.

Trixie nodded. "A vegetarian place called the Purple Turnip."

Eric paused thoughtfully, then said, "Yeah, I'll come. Can you wait about ten minutes while I shower and get pulled together?"

"Sure. We'll meet you in the lobby."

His acceptance took Trixie by surprise. She had hoped he would come, so she could keep an eye on him. But he looked so tired. *He really must be lonely,* she thought. Then something startling occurred to her.

Maybe he was coming so *he* could keep an eye on *her!*

An Evening to Remember • 10

DUSK WAS ALREADY FALLING as the group pulled into the charming little village of Groverville. Quiet streets and cozy homes encircled the parklike town square as if it were a magnet. At one end of the square was a picturesque New England church, its steeple silhouetted like a white spear against the darkening sky. Opposite the church was the old town meeting house, with the date *1799* over the doorway. Linda explained that it was still used for town meetings.

Trixie was most impressed by the huge old maples lining the streets. When those trees leafed in the spring, they would form a honeycomb of tunnels throughout the town.

Wanda pointed out a particularly gnarled old tree

in the center of the town square. "They say that's where Thomas Mead was hanged," she told them. "There's a statue nearby of the two men who captured him, but the hanging tree gets a lot more attention."

"Don't you think we should take them by the restaurant now while it's still light?" asked Linda. "Then we can go back and see Jenny."

Wanda agreed and steered the Tan Van along the river until they were out of town. They turned a corner and came to an old covered bridge. As the van rumbled over the wooden structure, Di sighed, "Isn't this romantic?" No one disagreed with her.

On the other side of the bridge were an old sawmill and barn. Both were blanketed with snow. "Everything looks just like a scene from a Christmas card!" exclaimed Trixie.

Wanda explained that the sawmill was no longer in use, but that it had been the one that provided the boards for the bridge. To the Bob-Whites' surprise, they discovered that the old barn was the Purple Turnip restaurant.

It was all but dark by the time they reached the Fleming home, though just light enough to see a white picket fence and snowman in the front yard, and a little girl running down the front walk toward the van, blond pigtails flying behind her. She was wearing blue jeans and a turquoise T-shirt. Her gait was awkward, but her smile was one of pure delight. She gave giant bear hugs to her sisters and sunny greetings to the rest of them.

"Come inside," she begged, tugging on Wanda's

hand. "Come on, the tea party's all ready!"

The inside of the house was simply furnished, although, like the Belden home, it was overflowing with years of accumulated Christmas decorations. On one wall were several neatly framed crayon scribblings. Trixie went over to look. Each picture was a combination of brilliant colors signed with a careful, though not always accurately spelled, "Jenny."

Jenny had them sit on the floor around a long low coffee table in the living room. In front of each of them was a doll-sized plate and teacup and a Christmas napkin.

The door from the kitchen opened, and a large-boned woman came out. She had short black hair that was turning steel gray at the temples and eyes that crinkled at the corners. Moving with the grace of a ballet dancer, she set her tray down near Jenny.

As the boys started to stand to greet her, she said, "No, please keep on sitting. I know how difficult it is to get up from that table! I'm Mrs. Fleming. I told Jenny that you were going to eat dinner right away and that it was too late for a tea party, but she insisted. I hope you don't mind."

"Not at all," Mart spoke up quickly. "We're in favor of eating any time."

"We're going to take them to the Purple Turnip, Mom," Linda said.

"Oh, good, then we aren't spoiling your dinner. Service is very slow there," Mrs. Fleming said, her eyes twinkling with laughter. "This tea party is special for Jenny. She has learned something very difficult, and when she found out you were coming, she chose this as her reward. Jenny, why don't you show off what you learned?"

Jenny ran back to the entryway, where all the boots and shoes were lined up, and grabbed a pair of tennis shoes. She came back and sat down on the floor in front of the fireplace. She put them on and slowly tied the lace on the right shoe into a bow.

"Oh, Jenny," Wanda breathed.

"Not done yet," Jenny cut her off. Then, with the same concentration, she tied her left shoelace.

Linda and Wanda jumped up and hugged their sister while everyone else clapped and cheered.

"Jenny, you little sneak!" cried Linda. "We didn't even know you were working on tying your shoes."

Jenny glowed under all the praise and approval.

"A tea party is the perfect celebration," agreed Wanda. "Shall I pour while you pass the cookies, Jenny?"

As Wanda poured the fruit punch, Jenny handed the platter of green-frosted Christmas-tree cookies to Mart. Mart politely took one and put it on his plate.

"You get two," said Jenny. "Everybody gets two."

"Terrific!" said Mart as he snatched another from the platter he'd already passed on to Eric.

"Did you help make these cookies, Jenny?" Eric asked, speaking up for almost the first time that evening.

She nodded proudly. "I got to help punch them out with the tree cutter and put the little red decorations on the top."

"They look very nice," said Eric. "I liked to make cookies when I was your age, too."

Somehow, Trixie thought, *Eric looks out of place sitting on the floor, drinking juice out of a doll's cup, and talking about baking cookies.*

After the group was done eating, Linda and Wanda insisted on doing the dishes. Jenny took Eric's hand and said, "Come see my new puzzle. I have lots of 'em." She led him to the dining room table where her puzzles were spread out.

The Bob-Whites settled on the floor around the fireplace and listened to Mrs. Fleming explain what it was like to have a handicapped child. She told them about the adjustments and sacrifices they had to make when they discovered that Jenny was handicapped, about Jenny's schooling and all that she was learning, and about the specialness of having Jenny as part of their family. "It's important for kids like Jenny to have friends, to feel loved and needed," she concluded.

"It's easy to see that you and your family are making her feel exactly that way," said Honey.

Mrs. Fleming smiled. "It's not hard to do."

Jenny and Eric came back into the living room. "You know, Mrs. Fleming, your daughter is one fantastic puzzle-putter-togetherer," Eric said. "She was showing me where the pieces go when I couldn't figure it out for myself."

"Some of her puzzles are a bit tricky if you're not familiar with them," Mrs. Fleming responded. "But she loves them and does very well with them. She even has her own puzzle company."

"What?" asked Trixie.

"Go get a couple of your puzzles, Jenny. My husband designs children's puzzles," Mrs. Fleming explained. "He cuts them out of wood, and we all help with the sanding. Then Jenny chooses the colors and paints the puzzle pieces, frequently without any assistance. They're called 'Jenzles' and are sold on consignment in several stores around the area. The money goes into Jenny's savings fund."

Jenny came in carrying a few brightly colored wooden puzzles in animal shapes and simple designs.

"What a neat gift for Bobby!" Trixie exclaimed. "Will you sell me the star puzzle, Jenny?"

"And I'll buy four more for my twin brothers and sisters," Di said enthusiastically.

"These are very easy puzzles," Mrs. Fleming reminded them. "They really are for preschoolers. How old are your brothers and sisters?"

"Bobby is the oldest and he's six," Trixie answered. "But that doesn't matter. The colors are so pretty it's like giving them a picture."

While Linda and Wanda wrapped the puzzles in leftover Christmas paper, the others thanked Mrs. Fleming and Jenny for the tea party.

Jenny vigorously shook hands with each of the Bob-Whites, and when she came to Eric, she added a shy hug and said, "Thank you for playing puzzles with me."

He gave her a small kiss on the cheek and said, "You're a very nice young lady, Jenny."

I don't get it, Trixie thought to herself once they

were back in the van. *Eric's so kind and gentle with Jenny; she obviously adores him. And kids, especially ones as sensitive as Jenny, seldom make mistakes about people. . . .*

Trixie lost her train of thought about Eric when she saw the interesting decor of the Purple Turnip. Inside the old barn, it was cozy and bright. All kinds of healthy plants were suspended from the open-beamed ceiling. Where the milking stalls had been, a bustling kitchen now existed. People were actually working behind stanchions that had once held cows in place.

An assortment of tables covered the main floor and the small loft. Some were old kitchen tables, some were ornate tables that could have come from the Wheelers' formal dining room, and some weren't really tables at all, but other things converted into tables. In a far corner, the Bob-Whites found a large table that had apparently been the door to the old barn. It had plenty of room for everyone, so they claimed it.

Trixie gazed around and saw that nothing matched. The cloth place mats and napkins were all different colors and designs, the dishes were of various types of pottery, and the chairs were equally incongruous.

Honey picked up her knife, fork, and spoon. Each was a different pattern. "This reminds me of dinner at the Belden house when it's Mart's turn to set the table," she giggled.

"Great minds can't be bothered with such trivia when contemplating loft-ier considerations"—Mart waved toward the loft in an unnecessary attempt to get his pun appreciated—"namely, the food one *eats* with these various implements."

As if on cue, a waitress came over to their table and handed each of them a menu. "It's an interesting menu," she informed them. "Here are some sunflower seeds to munch on while you read it." She set a pottery bowl in the middle of the table.

"That's her way of saying it will be a long time before she'll be back to take our order," Linda explained good-humoredly. "We have to suffer through reading about terrific-sounding foods, meanwhile contenting ourselves with seeds and water."

Trixie, sitting across from Eric, watched him carefully. He kept fidgeting and tapping his fingers. Almost as soon as he picked up his menu, he put it down again.

"Have you decided already?" she asked him.

"Yeah, I guess I'll just have the special. The menu's too long to bother reading."

"Mushroom goulash—that does sound good," agreed Jim. " 'Mushrooms sautéed with nuts, tomatoes, water chestnuts, celery, green onion, and Chinese peapods, topped with grated cheese. Served with a green salad and a choice of beverage.' Mmmm . . . I can't decide between that and the vegetarian pizza."

"Everything is tasty here," Wanda said. "Mart, are you finding anything you like?"

"The cheese lasagna is whispering sweet nothings to my taste buds," Mart admitted.

Trixie laughed. "Lasagna ranks right after hamburgers with Mart. He can eat it by the panfuls. I'm tempted by the eggplant Parmesan myself."

"The cheese and bean sprout sandwich with the

bowl of lentil soup sounds about right for me," said Honey.

"I could go for some vegetable chop suey," Brian decided.

The waitress did not return until long after the sunflower seeds were gone and the menus had been read and reread. But the food turned out to be well worth the long wait, and the portions were giant-sized. Di offered to trade bites with anyone who wanted a taste of her avocado soufflé, which led to a bite-swapping circus.

"A veritable vegetable feast" was the verdict from Mart. "Wanda, you've won your bet. Meat is not required for a palatable meal!"

"The Purple Turnip will fit right in with a natural resort on Mead's Mountain, don't you think?" Linda asked.

Everyone agreed immediately.

In the midst of an argument over ordering zucchini cake or frozen yogurt for dessert, Trixie looked up and exclaimed, "Why, Miss Trask! Pat, Katie, what are you doing here?"

"It was rather impulsive," said Miss Trask. "Katie was telling me what an interesting restaurant this is, and Pat said that it's better to show than to tell, so here we are."

"I'm so glad you came," said Honey. "The food is delicious, almost as good as yours is, Katie."

"Oh, we've already eaten," explained Katie. "Pat cooked one of his specialties tonight. Actually, he's a better cook than I am. We just came to get some dessert and to listen to the music."

The Bob-Whites pushed their chairs closer together to make room for the newcomers.

"Is Rosie holding down the fort out at the lodge all by herself?" asked Brian.

"That little rabble-rouser could bring down the entire mountain in five minutes flat by herself," Pat chuckled. "No, the honeymooners offered to watch her."

"I didn't know people on their honeymoon liked to baby-sit," Di said. "I thought they were just supposed to want to be alone together."

Miss Trask smiled. "It seems the man is an English teacher, and there's a special showing of *Macbeth* on TV tonight that he told his students to watch. The only television set at the lodge is in Pat and Katie's apartment."

"It really worked out nicely," said Katie. "We rarely have a chance for an evening out with adults, or even teen-agers!"

After the waitress had taken their dessert orders, Pat commented, "This seems to be where the action is for Mead's Mountain people. I saw Bert and Jack over by the door as we came in."

"Really?" asked Trixie.

"Why don't we invite them to join us, too?" suggested Honey. "There's enough room to add two more chairs."

Bert and Jack brought over their pots of herbal tea and seemed happy to join them. "How are things with the famous junior detectives?" hailed Bert. "I suppose you're on the trail of the ghost of Mead's Mountain."

At that moment, the waitress arrived with their desserts, and in the confusion, Trixie managed to say, "Not at all," and leave it at that. She could hardly accuse Eric of anything when he was sitting right across from her.

An older man with gray wavy hair and a thick moustache came up to their table to greet Linda and Wanda. "Glad to see you're back in town instead of hibernating out in the mountains," he said.

"Jim Carlyle!" Linda exclaimed. She pointed to the guitar case in his hand. "You're not the music tonight, are you?"

"Sure am."

"Marvelous! These are some of our friends . . . here's another Jim, Jim Frayne. His father might buy Mead's Mountain and turn it into a natural resort area."

"What a great idea," Jim Carlyle said heartily.

Wanda introduced the others at the table and explained, "Jim is the music teacher at the high school, as well as an old family friend. We have an evening of good music ahead of us!"

Wanda had not exaggerated. Jim Carlyle played the guitar beautifully and sang many old folk songs in a warm, mellow voice. Everyone in the crowded restaurant, even the waitresses and waiters, chimed in at the choruses. All too soon, the evening of music ended with a medley of Christmas carols that caused even the cooks in the kitchen to join in the singing.

"I hope someone is good at math," their waitress announced when she brought their check. "I guess

I shouldn't have put everything on one bill. It might be confusing to divide up."

"No need to," said Eric, reaching for the bill. "I'll take care of it."

"No, we'll each take care of our own share," Trixie protested. "It's more fair that way."

"I said I would pay the bill," he answered. Something in his manner made Trixie give up her arguing. "I guess the Christmas carols got me into a generous mood," added Eric. "Besides, vegetables don't cost very much."

As everyone thanked him, Trixie wondered how a college student who had to work during Christmas vacation could afford such moods of generosity . . . *unless it was because of money from Wanda's quarters and Honey's watch.*

Pat stood up. "It's time Katie and I left. We've got to be up early to get the lodge in action, and if any others at this table are interested in keeping their jobs, they can hop on the O'Brien train, too."

Linda, Wanda, and Eric all took Pat up on his offer and left in his pickup truck. Soon Bert and Jack took off in their small rented car.

Only the Bob-Whites and Miss Trask stayed on, to linger over their cups of herbal tea and enjoy the peaceful darkness of the restaurant, a darkness punctured only by candlelight.

A Brush with Death • 11

THE RAIN HAD CHANGED to crusty snowflakes and the wind had picked up by the time the Bob-Whites and Miss Trask came out of the restaurant and piled into the Tan Van. As they were heading back to the lodge, Jim suggested a midnight swim. Everyone was in favor of it except Trixie, whose short night's sleep was beginning to hit her, and Miss Trask.

"I don't know where you get all your energy," Miss Trask sighed. "Tomorrow morning is soon enough for my swim." She swung the Tan Van from the highway to the narrow road that went to the lodge.

Trixie listened to the wind as it whipped the treetops back and forth and howled through the gullies of the mountainside, creating an eerie song: *hurry home, Bob-Whites, hurry home.* She shook herself awake and tried to concentrate on the conversation.

"You know, something should be done with this road," Jim was saying. "It's been carelessly cut into the side of this mountain, leaving the exposed area open to erosion. Look how some of the trees are already starting to lean over the roadway."

"Let's put that into our notes for Mr. Wheeler," Brian said.

After Miss Trask had to slow down to negotiate another hairpin corner, she commented, "This road would be a lot safer if it were straightened out—"

Before she could finish, a loud *s-s-n-nap* filled the air. While the others peered out their windows to locate the source of the sound, Miss Trask stepped on the gas, and the van lurched forward. Suddenly something brushed against the back of the van, and they looked back in time to witness a large tree crashing directly behind them, its outer branches actually touching the van.

As the others gasped in horror, Miss Trask slammed on the brakes and pulled the van over to the side of the road. "Thank heavens for quick reflexes," she said, trying to sound matter-of-fact. "I could tell that was coming, but I wasn't sure I'd be able to react in time."

"You're certainly more alert than any of us," Honey breathed gratefully.

"Come on, Brian," said Jim. "Let's get that thing off the road so cars can get through tomorrow."

Trixie, more wide-awake than she'd been for hours, grabbed a flashlight out of the glove compartment and got out of the van to take a look around. A gust of wind hit her in the face as she joined Jim and Brian near the fallen tree.

"This is way too big for us to pull off the road," Brian decided, taking the flashlight and running it down the length of the tree. "Pat's going to have to get a chain saw down here. Wait till Mr. Wheeler hears about how far the erosion has gone."

"Just a minute," Trixie whispered hoarsely. "Look at this." She pointed to the trunk end of the tree.

"It's been sawed!" Jim exclaimed.

Trixie shivered. "The note—the note said my life was in danger! Let me have that flashlight a minute." She explored the area around the trunk and discovered a mass of footprints there in the snow.

Miss Trask's voice came to them through the blowing snow. "Do you need more help back there?"

"We'll be right there," Jim called back.

"Here's a whole perfect footprint, and another," Trixie said tensely. "They go off in this direction. Let's follow them!"

Miss Trask called again. "We must get back to the lodge before the storm gets worse."

"Whoever it was is long gone by now, Trixie," Jim said. "Come on, we're not doing any good standing around in the storm all night. Let's not mention this to Miss Trask for now. We don't want to alarm her."

It was a silent group that traveled the rest of the way to the lodge. Trixie, deep in thought, again seemed to hear the wind singing its song.

"I'm going to report the tree to Pat and Katie," said

Miss Trask as they got out of the van. "I'd advise the rest of you to skip your midnight swim and go right to bed."

Mart was the first to enter their suite. Just inside the door, he stooped to pick up something from the floor, nearly causing Trixie to tumble directly over his back. "What are you doing, Mart?" she complained. "Trying to make me break my leg?"

Mart turned and gave her a peculiar look. "We'd all be a lot safer if you did," he said.

"What in the world are you talking about?"

"Would you like to tell us what you and Brian and Jim found in the woods?" Mart countered.

"That falling tree was no accident," admitted Jim. "It had been sawed through and pushed over as we went by."

"That's about what I expected," said Mart grimly. He held out a folded piece of white paper. "It's got your name on it, Trixie."

Trixie took the note and read the by now familiar red block letters:

NEXT TIME I WON'T MISS

T.L.M.

"Oh, no," Honey gulped. She jumped up and hugged Trixie. "What are we going to do?"

Mart shook his head. "If Miss Trask knew about this, she'd have us packed up and on the next flight out of here."

"I've been thinking about that," Brian spoke up. "If Trixie really is in danger, Miss Trask should know.

Especially since we don't have any idea who T.L.M. might be."

"Brian, I am not in any real danger," said Trixie stubbornly. "Someone is just trying to distract us from the moonshining or whatever is going on here. And don't you dare mention that to Miss Trask. You'll worry her to death, and we'll never get to the bottom of this. Anyway, we have an excellent clue as to who T.L.M. is."

"We do?" They all stared at her blankly.

"The footprints near the tree," she said. "They were man-sized waffle-stomper boot prints."

Brian threw his hands up in the air. "Everyone at the lodge wears waffle stompers," he said. "That's what you *wear* in mountains like these, Trixie."

"Let's check our own boots to compare the patterns on the bottom," said Trixie.

All of their boots turned out to have the same design of several bars around the outside of the boot. But Di's had crosses in the center and Jim's had chevrons, while everyone else's had four-pointed stars.

"I suppose you remember what our tree trimmer had for footprints," said Mart skeptically.

"Of course," Trixie answered. "They had stars with five points in the center."

"So all we need to do," said Honey, "is find someone with man-sized waffle stompers that have a five-pointed star design, and we have our ghost!"

Trixie disagreed. "All I need to do," she said, "is get some sleep!"

By morning, the wind was gone and the sun reigned

over the skies again. After breakfast and their swim, the Bob-Whites asked Katie to make a picnic lunch so they could spend the entire day in the mountains. At the base of the chair lift, they stopped to talk to Pat, who was operating the lift.

"I called the road crew last night," Pat told them. "They cleared away the tree the first thing this morning. I sure am glad you kids didn't get hurt."

"Yes, that *would* have cramped our skiing style today," Mart observed.

"Which way are you headed?" Pat asked.

"Into the valley on the other side of this ridge," Brian replied. "We were looking at the relief map in the lobby, and that area seems to have lots of small up-and-down knolls."

Pat grinned. "It should be good skiing. But then, most places around here are."

"Everything is so lovely," raved Di. "You're lucky to live here year-round."

"Yes, it's been wonderful," he said. Then he sighed. "It's rough to find the perfect place to live and the perfect life-style, only to be forced to give them up. I know we'll never find another place to match this." He made a sweeping gesture toward the lodge and mountains.

"Are you moving, then?" asked Trixie.

"I guess we don't really have much choice. Don't you kids feel bad about it. It's not your fault, and there's nothing you can do. I guess there's nothing anyone can do. I only hope that we can save enough money for a down payment on a farm before we have to leave." Abruptly, Pat left them to help some other skiers get on the chair lift.

"How about that!" Trixie exclaimed, once the lift was in action. "He's moving because he's being forced to."

"What could be wrong?" Brian wondered.

"He said it's not our fault," added Di. "Now, why would it be our fault?"

"Somebody wants him out of here," Trixie conjectured after a moment's reflection.

"Do you think he's being blackmailed?" asked Honey.

"It sounds kind of like it," Trixie said thoughtfully. "Or else he could be running from something. Maybe he did something terrible, and now he's being forced to leave—jeepers! If he is in some kind of trouble, he sure wouldn't want a bunch of detectives here at the lodge."

"I see what you mean," Mart said. "It would be very easy for Pat to be the one playing ghost."

"I find that extremely hard to believe," Jim said curtly. "Pat and Katie O'Brien are two of the nicest people I ever met. They're always cheerful and helpful. When I told Pat about the deer we saw when we were skiing, he explained how he puts feed out for them and how they're almost tame now. A man like that doesn't go around doing the kind of things our ghost has been doing."

"But he sure has some kind of a problem," Trixie said, "and it sounds to me like he's in trouble."

"Maybe," said Jim as they all stepped off the lift.

"But let's just keep alert and not jump to any conclusions. Okay?"

"I've just been adding it up," Mart groaned. "In between keeping an eye on the O'Briens, Eric, and Mr. Moonshine and looking for Honey's watch, we won't be able to do our job and earn our car expenses."

"Oh, yes, we will," said Brian. "That's the most important thing. And let's get started, right now."

They spent the entire morning crisscrossing the mountainside on crooked trails and through open fields. Near noon, they came to a small clearing on the edge of a gentle cliff. Before them stretched a panoramic view of the entire valley.

Honey gazed down in appreciation. "It's places like this that make you realize that this world is certainly a beautiful place to live," she sighed.

"At the risk of disturbing your pastoral reverie," Mart said, "might I add that this looks like the perfect place for lunch?"

"We've earned it," agreed Jim. "This cross-country skiing is hard work. I'm glad we all keep in good shape." He dropped down to the ground, looking like he was in anything but good shape.

As Honey and Brian started getting out the fried chicken and fruit, Di took a small sketch pad out of her pack. "I have to have twenty-five good sketches for my art class by the end of the semester," she said. "Trixie, may I sketch you staring out into the valley?"

"Sure, how's this?" Trixie puffed out her cheeks and stood on one leg, stretching her other leg and arms straight out.

"I think it's stunning," Di said wryly, "but I doubt Mr. Crider would agree. Just keep on sitting on that rock and looking out into the valley as you were. I like that profile view. I'll be done in just a couple of minutes."

Jim came over to watch while Di made quick, precise strokes. "How's Mr. Crider as a teacher, Di? I'm thinking of taking art appreciation from him next semester."

"I like him a lot. He's a good teacher and really knows his stuff. If you do take it, you won't be bored."

"You seem to know your stuff, too. You're really quite good."

"Thank you, Jim, but I'm not that good," said Di with a pleased smile. "I do enjoy art, though, and I'm thinking of majoring in it at college. That is, if I can ever get out of high school!"

Jim grinned. "You'll do fine, Di. You're much smarter than you think you are."

Trixie, trying to sit still for Di, caught some movement out of the corner of her eye. "Honey!" she croaked. "Look down there! Isn't that Mr. Moonshine—skiing out of control?"

Below them, the old man twisted frantically through the trees, heading at an alarming speed for the bottom of the hill.

An Accident—and a Warning • 12

"He looks like a movie that's been speeded up," Honey fretted.

"He's either training for the Olympics or else he's missing all those trees by pure chance," said Trixie.

The old man's luck ran out when he tried to swerve around a large birch. His skis slid over to the side, and he tumbled head first into the tree.

Honey screamed, and Trixie yelled for the other Bob-Whites. Seeing the still heap Trixie was pointing to, Jim and Brian quickly reached for the first aid kit and started climbing straight down. Trixie was already slipping and sliding down to the old man. Honey, Di, and Mart came straggling along behind Jim and Brian.

Although the sight of blood normally didn't bother Trixie that much, she felt her stomach turning queasy. The man was lifelessly wrapped around the tree, sticky redness oozing from his head into the clean white snow.

Brian came up and immediately dug into the kit for some sterile bandages to cover the cut. Then he applied pressure to stop the bleeding.

"Oh, Brian, is he . . . is he alive?" asked Trixie in a quavering voice.

"Very much so," said Brian. "It's probably not as bad as it looks. It's a head wound, which always bleeds a lot even when it isn't very deep."

The old man moaned.

"Don't move," warned Brian. "Where does it hurt?"

"My head," he muttered, so faintly Brian could barely hear.

"Anywhere else?" Brian asked as he felt for broken bones.

"No . . . I don't think so," said the man haltingly.

"I don't think there are any internal injuries," Brian reported.

Trixie and Jim had spread their windbreakers out on the snow, and together they all carefully laid the old man on them. Then the others took off their windbreakers and sweaters to wrap around him. "We should keep him as warm as possible so he doesn't go into shock," said Jim.

"That may not be easy in this snow," said Brian, gently wiping the blood off the man's face.

"Should I get the windproof blankets in our survival

kits?" Honey asked. "And maybe something warm to eat?"

Everyone looked at her in astonishment. "Honey, you sure can keep your head in an emergency," said Jim.

Honey glowed as she and Di started back up the cliff. Not too long ago, she would have been the first to faint at the sight of blood. Now she was actually helping in a big way.

The old man whispered something weakly as the rest of them waited for Di and Honey to return with the food and blankets.

"It's only a shallow gash on the side of your forehead," Brian told him. "The kind that might give you a headache for a few days. You're very lucky, sir."

Mr. Moonshine just grunted. To Trixie, it didn't sound like a grunt of agreement.

"I'm going to pack cold snow around your cut now," Brian said soothingly. "That should help stop the bleeding and some of the pain."

The old man simply moaned his consent.

Soon Honey and Di came puffing back. "Getting back up that cliff isn't easy, but we found a less steep path not too far away," said Di. "How is he?"

"He seems to be okay," Brian assured them. "He could use something to drink, though."

"Katie packed a container of tomato soup," recalled Honey. She poured a cup for the old man. "Here, sir, this will help you keep warm. You remember Trixie and me from yesterday, don't you?" she said, and then she introduced the others.

The old man, with trembling hands, took a few sips, then looked up. He seemed to study each of them, his gaze resting on Brian. "My name's Carl," he said weakly. "Just Carl, that's all. I feel better now." He started to sit up slowly.

Trixie could tell that his head still really hurt, but he seemed determined to get moving.

"You need to rest," Brian said. "Some of us will ski back to the lodge for a rescue litter. Then we'll take you to a hospital. You should be examined by a professional."

"You're professional enough for me. I'm a tough old coot."

"Are you sure you're okay, sir? You really ought to have that cut cleaned and bandaged by a doctor," Brian worried. "You may need stitches."

"No, I don't break easy. You just fix me up the best you can, young man. You're a—a nice bunch of kids." Carl's voice trailed off, then he seemed to gather strength. "Listen and listen closely. To thank you for helping me, I've got some important advice for you. Mead's Mountain is a nice place to ski, but playing detective games here may not be very healthy. I'm telling you this because . . . I don't want to see you hurt."

"How do you know we're detectives?" asked Trixie.

"Word gets around. I'm just telling you to play it safe and mind your own business."

Brian began bandaging the head wound as well as he could. "Let's not worry about that now. The important thing is to get you somewhere warm where you can rest. Where do you live? We'll help you home."

"No!" Carl tried to get to his feet, but he sank back to the ground in pain. "Just let me rest here. I'll be fine."

"Here, have something to eat, Carl," Di urged. "How about a chicken leg?"

After Carl had eaten some chicken and drunk more soup, he managed to stand up. "I have work to do," he said awkwardly. "Thank you for your help."

"Are you *sure* you're okay?" Brian asked again. "We'd be happy to help you to wherever you're going."

"I'm fine," he snapped. "How many times do I have to tell you that! Will you kids just quit meddling in my life?" Then he pointed at Trixie and yelled, "Especially you!" With that, off he skied into the woods.

"Wow, Trixie! He *is* a bit peculiar, your Mr. Carl Moonshine," said Jim.

"Peculiar, nothing. He's a moonshiner or my name isn't Trixie Belden."

"Okay, Elizabeth Taylor," said Mart, "let's discuss it while we finish lunch."

"Please, not here," said Di, pointing to the blood-stained snow.

"You're right," agreed Mart. "This place diminishes even my appetite."

"Come on," Jim said, "we have to go back up the cliff anyway to get our skis and stuff."

Soon they were all settled comfortably, eating the remains of their lunch and admiring the panoramic view below them.

"Now," said Trixie, "let's go over all the clues."

"I'm totally mixed up," Honey admitted. "There's so much going on—Carl, Eric, Pat, the ghost, and those awful notes."

"All we can do about Eric or Pat is check their footprints," said Trixie. "It's Carl who's really mystifying."

"I didn't like his warning about Mead's Mountain being unhealthy," said Jim. "Especially after that last note."

"Eric must have told him we're detectives," Trixie reasoned. "They're up to something, otherwise they wouldn't be worried about our being detectives."

"You're jumping to conclusions, Harriet Beecher Stowe," Mart taunted.

"In spite of his odd remarks, there's something about Carl that I like," said Brian thoughtfully. "He does seem to be a tough old coot."

Trixie was astonished. "Gleeps, Brian, he was downright rude, and after you practically saved his life. He didn't want us around any more than necessary. Look how he acted when you suggested taking him home—like we were poison!"

"I didn't save his life at all," Brian sighed. "Besides, people who love the mountains and live there alone for a long time can forget normal courtesies."

"People who love the mountains don't keep all their shades pulled down in the middle of the day," Trixie retorted. "I know something funny is going on in there. That's why he didn't want us to take him home. He's probably on his way back from making a delivery of moonshine right now!"

Brian, Mart, and Jim groaned in unison.

"It's just too heavy for an old man, Trixie," said Brian. "Alcohol is used for other things besides drinking, you know. Doctors use a lot of it for sterilizing, for instance. You yourself said you used it in biology."

"Something that smells like alcohol is used in developing pictures, too," added Mart. "That, my dear Eleanor Roosevelt, would explain why the shades were closed."

"Oh. . . ." Trixie could see that her theory was evaporating into nothingness.

"Alcohol is also used in printing," Honey recalled. "I remember reading that some printers could become addicted to the smell of ink because of its alcoholic content."

"I did notice that his fingers were ink-stained, when I took his pulse," said Brian.

Trixie's face brightened. "Really?" Then she was silent as she sat on the snow-covered log, elbows resting on her knees, chin cupped in her hand, and her brow furrowed.

Mart bit into his second apple and tapped Trixie on the shoulder. "Oh, Virginia Woolf," he teased, "are we to deduce from your inertia that you've developed another perspicacious hypothesis with which to confound us?"

"I don't know," Trixie sighed. "I was just remembering that show we saw on TV last fall. The one about the huge black market in phony passports, driver's licenses, birth certificates, and other identifications. Wouldn't these mountains be a perfect place for that kind of work? You could have all your materials laid out and not worry about anyone interrupting you."

"I remember that show," Brian said. "But we have no reason to suspect Carl of having anything to do with false ID's."

"Why wouldn't he tell us his full name then?" asked Honey. "And why was he so rude, both now and when Trixie and I went to the cabin?"

"And why did his cabin smell of alcohol?" added Trixie. "Why are his fingers ink-stained?"

"I think I can answer all those questions," Di spoke up quietly.

There was a moment of silence as the others stared at Di in amazement.

"The art museum benefit my folks had last spring," Di said by way of explanation.

"Yes?" prompted Trixie.

"There were a lot of Carl Stevenson prints there, and we talked to his daughter, Ellen Johnson, for a while," Di continued. "She showed us one print of an old man with long white hair, called 'Legend of a Mountain Man.' She said it was really a self-portrait of her father, who lives alone in the mountains. It looked just like Mr. Moonshine."

"Di, you're right!" exclaimed Honey. "How thrilling to think that we may have actually met Carl Stevenson himself!"

"Of course you're right," said Jim. "The ink-stained fingers and artistic temperament. And the printer's ink smell in his cabin. That would also explain why he doesn't like a bunch of people around."

Trixie didn't say anything. She couldn't remember the picture very well at all. She was excited about having met a famous artist, but part of her was disappointed that he wasn't a backwoods moonshiner.

"That takes care of that," said Mart, standing up. "Now, if everyone's done eating, let's get off the wild-goose trail and back on the ski trail. Coming, Your Majesty, Queen of England?"

Trixie glared at him and sputtered, "Well, you're certainly no king, Mart Belden. You're not even a prince or—or a very nice brother!"

Jim laughed. "However that may be, I think we should head back to the lodge. It looks like a dandy storm is brewing."

Some Answers • 13

When the Bob-Whites got back to their suite, Pat, Katie, and Rosie were waiting for them with Miss Trask.

"Honey," said Miss Trask, "Pat and Katie have some news for you." Her tone of voice did not indicate whether the news was good or bad.

Katie gave Rosie a little shove toward Honey. "Tell her, Rosie."

Very shyly, Rosie went up to Honey. She held out her hand. In it was Honey's watch.

Honey squealed with delight. "Rosie! You found my watch!" She bent down and gave the girl a big hug. "Oh, you little darling!"

"Just a minute, Honey." Something in Pat's voice

made Honey stand up and look at him questioningly. "Go ahead, Rosie," he said. "Tell Honey the rest of the story."

In a quivering whisper, Rosie said, "I—I took it." Then she turned, ran back to Katie, and hid her face in her mother's lap.

Katie automatically began to stroke the girl's soft black curls and continued the story. "The first morning you were here, Rosie came to your room to meet you. She walked in and saw all of you out in the swimming pool. She tried to go outside, but she couldn't get the patio door open."

"Rosie must have been the one to lock our door!" exclaimed Trixie. "She did it by accident, thinking she was unlocking the door."

Pat went on, "When she went into the bedrooms to see if anyone was there, she saw Honey's watch. She thought it was pretty, and she's wanted a watch since a friend of hers got one for Christmas. Rosie has a problem understanding that she can't have everything that she wants or likes."

Katie sighed. "We're really sorry for all the inconvenience and worry we've caused you. Aren't we, Rosie?" She pulled Rosie up to a standing position.

"I'm sorry," Rosie sniffed. "I won't ever touch your watch again." Tears rolled down her round cheeks.

Honey realized that it was very important for Rosie to understand that she had done something wrong, but her compassionate nature couldn't tolerate any more of the child's unhappiness. She hugged Rosie again and said, "It's okay, honey, someday you'll have a watch of your very own."

Trixie's mind was racing. She remembered the first time she had met Rosie—when she got a scolding for taking a jar of peanut butter she shouldn't have. *Jeepers, did I miss that clue!* she thought. *Eric even said he was looking for her outside our suite.*

"Wanda's quarters!" Trixie interrupted her own thoughts out loud. "Has anyone asked Rosie about Wanda's quarters?"

Everyone turned to stare at Trixie.

"Well, I mean, if she thought Honey's watch was pretty, maybe she thought Wanda's quarters were, too."

"We returned them a few hours ago," said Pat. "Trixie, you're some detective, you know that?"

"That's what I told you," said Katie. "She's even famous!"

Mart cleared his throat. "Not to put an end to our shamus's hour of glory," he said, "but how did you find out that Rosie had the watch and the quarters?"

"She's supposed to rest every day after lunch," said Katie. "Lately she's been sneaking out of her room, so I went in to check on her today. There she was on the floor, making stacks of quarters. We had quite a little chat, and then she showed me the watch. But—we really have to go now. I'm just so happy we found the watch while you're still here."

"This time I will give it to Miss Trask for safekeeping," promised Honey.

After the O'Briens had left and Miss Trask had gone to her room to put Honey's watch away, Jim leaned over to Trixie and said, "I guess this lets Eric off the hook."

"No, it doesn't."

Jim raised a questioning eyebrow.

"Maybe he's not a thief, but don't forget the funny conversation I overheard," Trixie explained.

Mart snorted. "And don't *you* forget, Miss Scarlett O'Hara, that the man you heard him talking with is one of the most respected artists in the country. And furthermore, don't you forget your disposition toward overemphasizing, exaggerating, and downright imagining anything even remotely suspicious!"

"Some Rhett Butler *you'd* make," giggled Di as Miss Trask came back into the room.

"Honey," Miss Trask said, "as soon as you discovered that you had worn your good watch by mistake, you should have brought it to me."

"You're right, as always," Honey said apologetically. "I'll try to be more careful next time."

"Now that we've solved the mystery of the missing timepiece," Mart broke in, "perhaps we could take some time out for dinner?"

Trixie and Honey fell behind the others as they walked over to the restaurant. "If Eric doesn't turn out to be the ghost, who do you think it could be?" Honey wondered.

"There're lots of people," Trixie said. "Carl for one. I still think he's up to something, famous artist or not. And he's the one I saw in the woods the night our room was broken into and the fire was doused. Pat's another one. He's certainly had the opportunity. And what about Jack Caridiff? He's always talking about ghosts."

"But Jack was with us when all the lights flickered in the lodge," Honey said.

"Oh, that's right. I still think it's Eric," said Trixie just before they joined the others at the table.

As they were finishing another excellent dinner, Katie came up to their table with an announcement. "Tomorrow is New Year's Eve, you know."

"Already?" exclaimed Di. "We couldn't have been here that long."

"Oh, yes," laughed Katie. "And my question is, would you like to help plan a big party for everyone at the lodge? We would hold it in the lobby."

"We'd love to help!" said Honey. The others agreed, and Katie handed out paper and pencils.

"I thought the boys could be in charge of food," she said. "Mart seems like a natural for that job. And you girls might be in charge of entertainment and decorations. We don't need anything fancy."

The storm Jim had predicted materialized soon after dinner. The wind built up strength and the snow came down harder as the Bob-Whites kept busy making lists of food, decorations needed, and entertainment possibilities. Mart suggested a show with people from the lodge doing different songs and stories from their regions. This idea met with great enthusiasm, although Trixie claimed he thought of it just so he could be master of ceremonies.

"We could sing some folk songs from the Hudson River valley," Jim recommended. "Perhaps Linda and

Wanda would sing songs about the Vermont Green Mountains, and Bert and Jack might do something from the sea. We could ask Jim Carlyle to come and sing, too. And to make sure that Mart doesn't steal the show with his clowning around, we'll make Di co-master of ceremonies."

It was quite late by the time they completed their party plans and went to bed.

When Trixie woke up the next morning, the snow was still coming down and the wind was still blowing hard, although the storm had lost some of its fury.

She jumped out of bed with a burst of energy, then shivered as her feet touched the cold wooden floor. "You'd think they'd carpet the bedrooms, too," she muttered to herself, pulling on blue jeans and a red pullover sweater.

Today's going to be super busy, she thought. Besides the party, there was all this fresh snow—perfect for checking people's footprints. She bent over Honey's bunk and quietly shook her. "Wake up, sleepyhead," she whispered.

"Don't listen to her," came Di's voice from the other bunk. "We need lots of sleep if we're going to stay up late and see in the new year."

"I'm sorry, Di," Trixie said. "I didn't mean to wake you."

"You didn't. I'm already back to sleep."

Honey sat up and stretched. "What are you so excited about that you want to get started so early?" she asked.

"We've got to go check footprints."

"No one else is up yet. There won't be any footprints to check," responded Honey, ducking back under the covers.

Trixie threw Honey's jeans at her. "Come on! Lots of people are up."

Trixie went out to the living room and put on her wool socks and waffle-stomper boots. When Honey was ready, they went to the lobby. Eric was already there, putting kindling into the fireplace.

"Morning," he said stiffly.

"Are you building a fire?" asked Trixie.

"What's it look like?" he answered, heading for the door.

"Do you need any help getting more logs?" Trixie asked sweetly.

He looked at her suspiciously for a moment, then said, "Sure, that'd be nice. I don't mean to be short-tempered. I didn't sleep very well last night. The storm bothered me." He held the door open for her.

Trixie felt a flash of guilt. It wasn't nice of her at all. It wasn't because she wanted to help that she was going out in the snow.

They ran out to the woodpile around the corner of the building, where the wood was piled high under a protective roof. As Eric stooped over to pick up some logs, Trixie glanced down at the footprints in the snow. There were her own—small, ornamented with four-pointed stars. And there were Eric's beside hers, much larger . . . and ornamented with four-pointed stars, too!

"Hold your arms out," Eric commanded.

"What?" Trixie had been so intent on the footprints she'd forgotten all about the wood.

"Haven't you ever carried wood before? Hold out your arms!"

Eric piled the wood into her outstretched arms, and she hurried back inside and dumped the wood onto the fireplace hearth. As she brushed the bark chips from her sweater, she shook her head in answer to the question in Honey's eyes. "Four-pointed stars," she whispered.

Eric came back in and arranged the logs on the pile of kindling in the fireplace. "Sorry I was kind of short with you out there, Trixie," he said. "I do appreciate your help. I guess I'm disappointed because the weather is going to cut down on the time I can spend in the woods today."

"Do you think the storm is going to let up at all?" asked Honey.

"It has already," said Eric. "Matter of fact, Katie was saying she thought it might clear up by lunch, so that she and Miss Trask could go into town to do the shopping for the party."

"Come on, Honey, we'd better get back and wake up the others," said Trixie. "We have a lot of work to do before the party, ourselves."

On their way back to the suite, Honey declared, "That really clears Eric of everything. He's not the ghost, and he didn't take my watch or Wanda's quarters."

"There's still something odd about him," replied Trixie. "But I think I know who the ghost might be."

"Who?" asked Honey, not at all surprised that Trixie was already on the track of someone new.

"Carl. He knows we're detectives. He even warned us that being detectives here was unhealthy."

"Maybe it's time we took heed of that warning," sighed Honey as she opened the door to their suite.

The others were all up and dressed, sitting around the fire. "Ah, our early-morning peripatetics have come to roost," Mart said. "Feel like journeying to breakfast?"

"Someone should call the police and pawnshop," decided Miss Trask, "to let them know the watch has been returned."

"I will," volunteered Trixie. "Eric says you're going to town to do the party shopping with Katie this afternoon."

"Does Katie think the snow will let up by then?" asked Miss Trask. "Maybe I should go talk to her."

"Why don't you do that now?" Honey suggested. "We'll make our phone calls and meet you in the restaurant in about ten minutes."

After Miss Trask left, Trixie told the others about Eric's footprints.

"Well," said Brian, "I guess that takes care of Eric. But someone is still playing ghost around here, and I'd like to know who it is and why."

Di spoke up. "A lot of the evidence is beginning to point to Pat."

"He's so nice, though. It hardly seems possible," said Trixie.

"You're just saying that because last night he said

you were a good detective," gibed Mart. "I think we should check his footprints."

"Okay, but right now I'd better make those phone calls, so we won't be late meeting Miss Trask," said Trixie, reaching for the phone.

Trixie called the police, and then she called Pawnbroker Joe and told him the watch had been found at the lodge. She didn't say that Rosie had taken it and let the talkative pawnbroker assume that Honey had simply misplaced it.

"I'm right glad to hear that," he said. "I was worried about your little friend thinking Vermont was full of crooks. It seems like we're getting more and more hoodlums up here every day. A body even has to lock his doors at night now. It's shameful. That's just what I was telling the police when they came here to warn me about the counterfeit money this morning."

Trixie tried to interrupt to ask him what he was talking about, but his flow of words didn't stop. "You know, in my business you meet a lot of shady characters," he continued. "I try to run a good honest business to help people get a little money in times of need, but some of the folks I run into! The stories I could tell you—well, you're too young to want to know anything about shady characters and crooks. I'm just glad your friend found her watch and that it wasn't stolen by a Vermonter."

Finally he paused, and Trixie asked quickly, "What counterfeit money?"

"Counterfeit money? Oh, yes . . . what the police were talking about. Apparently someone passed some pretty good counterfeit twenty-dollar bills in town the other day. The bank caught them later. The police are telling all of us merchants in town to keep an eye out for them. They're supposed to be regular works of art, but the paper feels a little bit different from normal money. Maybe you'd better mention it to Pat O'Brien—isn't he the one in charge of the ski lodge out there?"

"Yes, he is," answered Trixie. She thanked him, hung up, then told the others about the conversation. "And I already know who the counterfeiter is," she finished.

Mart got down on the floor and salaamed Trixie. "You're clairvoyant!"

Trixie pretended to kick at him. "Get up, silly. If you had half a brain, you'd have already figured out who the counterfeiter is, too."

"First you physically brutalize me," Mart howled, "then you insult my mentality!"

"You're putting us on, Trix," said Jim. "You must have supernatural powers if you know that already."

"Are you sure this isn't another one of your famous hasty conclusions?" asked Brian.

Even Honey and Di were looking doubtfully at her.

"If I told you who it is, you'd all know I'm right," Trixie retorted. "But since you're being so awful, I won't tell you a thing. All I'll say is that I'll have you convinced I'm right before the year's out!"

Evidence! • 14

After breakfast, the Bob-Whites asked Katie where Pat was, hoping he'd be outside so they could check his footprints.

"Pat's in the apartment working on the account books," Katie told them. "It's such a miserable day that he decided to stay inside and get the bookwork done. If you want to talk to him, I'm sure he'd love an interruption."

Trixie shook her head. "We, uh, were just wondering if the ski lift was going to be operating today."

"Not unless the weather gets better," said Katie. "Then he might open it this afternoon. Listen, if you want something to do, I need a couple of gallons of ice cream made. We can store it outside until the party. And the decorating can be started anytime."

The boys went to the kitchen to make the ice cream, and the girls began hanging crepe paper streamers from the lobby ceiling. Di was unraveling the last roll of paper as Bert and Jack strolled into the lobby.

"Hi, girls," said Bert. "What's the good word?"

"Balloons," Trixie called from the top of the step-ladder. "We were just about to blow some up. Want to help?"

"Sure," said Bert. He took a balloon from Honey, and between puffs, he asked, "Have you girls seen Pat? We wanted to ask him about the weather conditions."

"He's doing some paper work," said Honey.

"It might clear up this afternoon," added Trixie. "They'll start the ski lift if it does. Vermonters sure know how to recover from snowstorms. Katie was expecting the roads to be okay by this afternoon, so she and Miss Trask could go shopping in town."

"Oh? Well, they've got that four-wheel-drive pick-up truck," Bert said. "It can go anywhere, snow or no snow."

"Say, how about singing some sea chanteys in the program tonight?" Trixie asked. "Or telling us about some of your adventures as merchant marines? We'd love to hear them."

"I don't think you'd better count on us," said Jack.

"What Jack means," said Bert, "is that we aren't very good singers. But if you want, we could work a little something up. Okay, Jack?"

"Well, sure, if you say so, Bert."

"I'm starved. I could use some lunch," Bert declared.

"We'll see you this evening, girls."

By the time the Bob-Whites had eaten lunch, the snow had almost stopped and the wind had completely died down. Miss Trask and Katie left for town, and the Bob-Whites decided to go back to the suite to work on their notes for Mr. Wheeler.

Trixie and Honey sat together on a couch in front of the fireplace. Trixie appeared to be deep in thought, and Honey finally leaned over and whispered, "You've got something on your mind, and I want to know what it is."

"I've been thinking about our first night here," Trixie said softly. "I think I've figured out how our ghost came in without leaving any footprints."

Honey looked startled, and Trixie explained, "He came in the front door, doused the fire, opened the patio door to make it look like he came in that way, and then went out the front door again, locking it behind him."

"But the front door was locked," Honey began. "Oh—you think Pat's the ghost instead of Eric. He would have had a key."

Trixie shook her head. "It doesn't matter. You don't need a key," she said smugly. "Honey, do you have your student ID with you—you know, the plastic-coated one?"

Honey fished the card out of her wallet, trying to control her curiosity.

"I'll go out in the hall, and you lock the door," Trixie commanded. "I'll be back in by the time you can count to ten."

Honey locked the door behind Trixie and began to count. "One . . . two . . ."

Trixie took Honey's card and slipped it in between the door and the doorjamb.

"Five . . . six . . ."

She forced the card against the lock and started to wiggle the card back and forth.

"Nine . . . ten . . ."

Trixie held on to the doorknob and tried to turn it, still wiggling the card.

"Thirteen . . . fourteen . . ."

Trixie was just about to ask Honey to let her in, when finally the door popped open! Trixie handed Honey her school card. "You count too fast," she breathed.

The other Bob-Whites were standing open-mouthed behind Honey.

"Trixie Belden, how did you do that?" Di asked in amazement.

"Cheap locks," Trixie answered. "Anyone with a credit card has a key to this door!"

"Dad's definitely going to have to replace those locks," said Jim firmly. "Here, let me try."

While the others took turns trying to open the locked door, Trixie grabbed Honey's arm and pulled her into their bedroom, closing the door behind them.

"I'm going back to the cabin in the woods," Trixie announced.

"I knew it," moaned Honey. "You *still* think Carl and Eric are guilty of something, don't you? Even though Eric isn't the ghost or a thief, and Carl is a famous artist, not a moonshiner."

"Everyone keeps forgetting about the conversation I overheard," said Trixie. "I do think they're up to something, and I think all the answers to this whole case lie in that cabin."

"You can explain it to me on the way," sighed Honey, reaching into the closet and pulling out her windbreaker. "There's nothing I can say that will change your mind."

Trixie gave her friend a hug. "I knew you'd come," she said.

"I don't have much choice—remember your promise that you wouldn't go anywhere alone? How about asking Jim to come, too?"

"I forgot about the promise," Trixie admitted. "But let's not ask Jim. We're only going to check footprints and look in a window if we can. There's nothing that can happen to us."

When the girls told the others that they were going for a walk, Brian said, "We might go skiing pretty soon. Think you'll be back in time?"

"Don't wait for us," Trixie said. "Where are you going?"

"Downhill—we want to explore what's below the lodge," said Brian.

"Have fun," said Honey. "We'll join you if we're here in time."

Trixie and Honey were delighted to see that Wanda had started the chair lift, which would save them a grueling walk up the mountain.

"The snow is kind of deep today," Wanda cautioned,

"but you won't have much of a problem. You kids have really gotten to be good cross-country skiers. One of these days you'll be showing up Rosie!"

After they had made the climb through the woods above the chair lift, Honey demanded that Trixie explain everything to her.

"You have to remember what the pawnbroker told me about the counterfeit money," Trixie began. "That's what really gave it away."

"What did he say?" prompted Honey.

"That the bills were works of art," replied Trixie.

"So?"

"Who would be better at making 'work of art' forgeries than an artist such as the best printmaker on the East Coast—Carl Stevenson!"

Honey stopped skiing. "But the man's a hermit, Trixie. He never goes to town. How could he have passed counterfeit money?"

"That's where Eric comes in," said Trixie. "Remember when Carl told Eric 'the money looks good'? He didn't mean they'd make a lot of money. He meant the money he made looks real!"

"Could be," murmured Honey as she started down the trail again.

"And do you remember the dinner we had at the Purple Turnip?" Trixie went on, ignoring Honey's doubtful tones. "Eric paid for that dinner with twenty-dollar bills. And remember how nervous he was."

Honey looked thoughtful. "I do remember that he was awfully quiet while the rest of us joked and laughed a lot."

"See? It all fits together!" Trixie cried triumphantly.

"Well, just a minute," Honey demurred. "It's very difficult to make a plate to counterfeit money. Carl would probably be able to do it, but he's such a well-known artist that he can make all the money he would ever want with his prints, which would be much easier to do."

Trixie hated to admit that what Honey said made sense. "Maybe he got tired of art and wanted to do something else. Maybe he considered counterfeiting a challenge," she said, making wild guesses. "I have a very strong feeling that he is a counterfeiter. And even if he isn't, we have to check his footprints to see if he's the ghost."

By this time, the girls had caught sight of the cabin. They stopped under a tree uphill from the cabin and took off their skis.

"I wish it were night," said Trixie. "If he's there and he glances out his window. . . ."

"You'd better get some story ready, just in case," warned Honey. "I don't think he'll buy the drink of water bit again!"

Trixie pointed to the back window of the cabin. The curtains were drawn, but there was a space of a few inches where they didn't quite meet. As silently as possible, the girls crept up to the window. Trixie pressed her face close to the glass. It was dirty, and the room was dark inside.

As Trixie's eyes slowly grew accustomed to the dimness, she could make out several printing presses and a lot of art material . . . and what looked like stacks of paper money on the table, and uncut sheets of money hanging to dry! She had her evidence!

Then Trixie heard Honey's muffled scream and felt a cold hand wrap itself around her neck.

"All right, detectives. Get inside," an icy voice commanded.

In the Cabin • 15

TRIXIE AND HONEY had no choice but to obey. They were forcibly pushed through the doorway, and the door was bolted behind them.

The girls stood shivering in what was obviously the living quarters of the cabin. There was a cot, a table, two chairs, a stove, an old-fashioned icebox, and nothing else, other than the pictures—Carl Stevenson pictures—that covered every spare inch of wall space. A piece of canvas divided the living section from the work area in back, where Trixie had seen the printing presses and the money.

Carl Stevenson shoved a second bolt across the door and turned toward them, his eyes flashing and his body trembling with anger. He had not changed the bandage that Brian had put on his head, nor had he bothered to wash the dried blood out of his white hair.

When he tried to talk to them, only sputtering came out, until finally he shook his fist at the ceiling and asked, "Why? *Why* does this have to happen now?"

Trixie was more than a little frightened. The idea of being locked in a cabin with a hermit often mistaken for a ghost was not appealing. She remembered the question that Honey had asked earlier, about why a man who could make so much money at art would want to counterfeit. Maybe because he was crazy—that's why! *And an old man living all alone in the mountains might easily go crazy,* Trixie thought. *Yipes! He might even believe himself to be Thomas Mead's ghost! Oh, why didn't we tell anyone where we were going?*

His face bright red, Carl moved toward Trixie and shouted, "What can I do with you?"

Behind her, Honey was shaking with fear, and Trixie knew that she had to act boldly.

"I suggest that you go to the police with us and turn yourself in," she said matter-of-factly. The calmness in her voice amazed her.

Carl went on as though he didn't hear her. "I can't just lock you in here until tonight. You'd be missed for sure. Then I'd have all those snoopy brothers of yours poking around here. No, that would never do."

Trixie tried again. "That's exactly why you should turn yourself in now," she said. "You haven't a prayer of escaping from all of us."

Carl paced the room and again acted as though

Trixie had not spoken. "If I let you go, you'd have the police swarming over this mountain so fast that everything would be ruined for sure. Why can't anything go according to plan? First my grandson shows up asking questions, then you meddle to the point of causing almost certain disaster." He turned on Trixie again and demanded, "I ask you, what should I do?"

"I told you. Go to the police with us and turn yourself in," Trixie repeated. "They're much easier on people who turn themselves in."

"Ha! Don't you think there's nothing I would like better? But I can't—Ellen's life depends on that!" All at once, the energy and anger seemed to drain out of Carl. He slumped down on the cot and shook his head. "Poor Ellen. Poor, poor Ellen!"

By now, Trixie was positive that Carl was crazy.

"Wh-Who's Ellen?" asked Honey.

"Ellen Johnson, my daughter . . . Eric's mother," he muttered.

"Eric's mo—of course! Eric is your grandson!" Trixie cried.

Carl continued to mutter. "When all this started, I *told* him to stay at school, but he's as stubborn as his mother was at that age."

"I'm really mixed up, Mr. Stevenson," said Honey. "I remember Eric saying that his mother was going to meet him here but had to go somewhere on business."

"Eric and his mother are very close. They're all each other has. Other than me, and I'm just an old man stuck out in the woods with his art. I always found that art understood me a lot better than people did.

So I guess I didn't try to understand people. I thought if Eric found out the truth about his mother, he'd go crazy with worry. But I was wrong. He's torn up inside, but he's acting mature on the outside and doing what has to be done."

"What *is* the truth about Ellen?" cried Trixie impatiently.

Carl looked at her, puzzled. "I thought Eric told me you kids were detectives. You mean to tell me you haven't got that figured out yet?"

"Something awful must have happened to her, but I don't know what," Trixie admitted.

"It's worse than awful."

"What happened?" urged Honey.

Carl sighed heavily. "About two weeks ago, I was peacefully carving on a wood-block print in my workshop. That's the back half of my cabin I caught you snooping around."

Trixie couldn't stop herself from blushing.

"Anyway, I heard a knock at the door. Well, that's pretty startling way out here. When I came out of the back room, my daughter was coming in the front door with two people wearing ski masks, really ugly masks. The tall one told me this wasn't a social call: They had kidnapped poor Ellen in New York."

Honey sucked in her breath.

"She was taking some new prints to an art dealer," Carl continued. "They followed her and forced her to bring them to see me. Their terms were simple. They hold her hostage until I make them a counterfeit plate and a large number of counterfeit bills. They warned me against calling the police."

"How terrible!" exclaimed Trixie.

"Is your daughter all right?" Honey asked.

"I don't know. She said she was okay when she was here. She even told me not to cooperate with their plans, but I have to, of course."

"Have you heard from her since then?" asked Honey.

Carl shook his head. "They said they were going to stash her away in the woods somewhere. I've been searching the woods every free minute, but I haven't seen a trace of her. The woods are so big, and there're so many places a person could be. . . ."

He looked so beaten and helpless that Trixie was gradually losing her fear of him. "So that's what that conversation was about," she said. "I overheard you telling Eric to search the woods and not to call the police. I'm sorry. I didn't really mean to be eavesdropping," she added quickly.

"That must have been the night I told Eric the truth about his mother. He was so concerned about her not telling him where she was going that I figured I owed him the truth."

"Do you know who the kidnappers are?" Honey queried.

"No, they always wear ski masks. There's a tall man with a harsh voice, and I can't recall the short one ever speaking. I couldn't even say if it's a man or a woman. At first Eric thought your gang might be the kidnappers, because you asked so many questions," said Carl, smiling vaguely. "But there's no doubt that the tall one is a full-grown man, and one who means business, too."

"Our 'gang' is called the Bob-Whites," Trixie announced, "and we're going to help you catch those criminals."

"I don't want to catch them. I just want to get my daughter back safely," said Carl.

"You're not going to let them get off scot-free?" asked Honey incredulously.

"Until Ellen's back, I want the police out of it. The kidnappers made it very clear that the police weren't to be involved."

"Tell us more about the kidnappers," Trixie requested.

"Well, they've come here a couple of times to see how the money plate is coming along. They never stay more than a few minutes and never say anything beyond a few new instructions. The tall one always does that. Once they saw me talking to Eric at the lodge. Probably the same night you overheard us. They figured out that he was Ellen's son." Carl sighed unhappily. "They decided that Eric should be the first to pass the money I made, so that if it wasn't good enough, he'd be the one to get caught. They came here early one morning and told me he was to pass some money as soon as possible. He wouldn't know who they were, but they'd be watching him. I gather that was the night he bought everyone dinner at the restaurant. Apparently the money worked okay."

Trixie shook her head. "The bank's discovered it."

"Oh, no!" Carl burst out. "I hope the kidnappers

don't know that." Then a surprised look came over his face. "How could they have detected the counterfeiting? It was perfect! The United States Mint couldn't have done a better job."

"The paper feels different," said Trixie.

"That explains it," he said. "The kidnappers brought me the paper."

"The police are telling merchants to watch out for twenties," Trixie said. Suddenly she was very glad she hadn't told Pat yet.

"What's the next move?" asked Honey.

Carl's face brightened. "Tonight I give them the plate and the counterfeit money and get my Ellen back."

"When? Where?" both girls breathed in unison.

"Eight o'clock at Porcupine Pond," he told them.

"Where's that?" Trixie asked.

"About five miles southeast of the ski lodge," Carl replied. "There's a trail forking off the road from the highway to the lodge that almost goes right there."

"Are you *sure* you don't want to let the police handle this?" asked Honey.

"Absolutely!" Carl insisted.

"Will Eric be there?" asked Trixie.

"No, I don't want him there in case anything goes wrong. If he knew about the meeting, he'd insist on coming, so I'm not going to even tell him about it."

"Nothing is going to go wrong, sir," said Trixie. "The Bob-Whites will see to that. You just be there with your money. After you have Ellen back safely, we'll take care of the kidnappers." Trixie wasn't exactly sure how they were going to accomplish that, but she knew they had to try.

"I don't want you to get mixed up in this," cried Carl. "You'll get hurt."

"Don't worry," Honey assured him. "You don't know Trixie."

Carl looked defeated. "Can I really trust you not to say anything to anyone until after the meeting?" he implored. "That's all I ask. If you give your word, I'll be happy to let you go."

"We'll only tell the other Bob-Whites," said Trixie. "We really want to help. You can count on us!"

Carl unbolted the door, and the two girls hurried outside. He watched anxiously as they ran to the tree where they'd left their skis. After they'd started back up the gully, they heard him call, "Remember—no police! And the kidnappers have guns!"

Suspects • 16

THE SKY WAS JUST TURNING purple by the time Trixie and Honey burst into the Bob-Whites' suite at the lodge. Di was drawing in her sketch pad, and the boys were back working on their notes for Mr. Wheeler.

"Hi! Where's Miss Trask?" Trixie asked carefully, trying to control her exuberance at all the news she had for them.

"She's in the kitchen helping Katie make dips for the party tonight," said Brian sternly. "That was some walk you took. You've been gone more than three hours."

"Is Miss Trask worried?" asked Honey.

Jim shook his head. "She got back just as we were returning from skiing. She asked about you and we said that you would be along shortly. You know Miss Trask—never interferes unless she's needed."

"You girls are hopping around like Mexican jumping beans," Brian said. "What have you been up to?"

"Oh, nothing," said Honey with an elegant wave of her hand. "It's just that Trixie has done exactly what she told us she was going to this morning."

"Corroborated the counterfeiter?" asked Mart. "As with other magic tricks, I'll believe this one when I see it!"

"Don't kid, Mart," begged Honey. "She really did find the counterfeiter—that is, the counterfeiter found us, only it's much more complicated than just that—Oh, you'd better explain, Trixie. I'm too excited!"

The Bob-Whites all listened in silence while Trixie spun her tale. "So you see," she concluded, "we just *have* to help Carl get his daughter back and catch the kidnappers."

"You are so gullible, Trixie!" Mart exploded. "Anyone can tell you a sob story and have you fall for it, no questions asked."

"What do you mean?" Honey demanded. "Don't you want to help?"

"Sure, if what Carl says is true. But did you ever stop to look at his story from any other viewpoint?"

"Like what?" asked Trixie.

"Like you've caught him red-handed and what else can he do?" suggested Mart. "He knows you'll go to the police if he lets you go, but he can't keep you there because he also knows your 'snoopy brothers' will come to your rescue. His only chance is to escape with the evidence. But how can he do that with you there? Of course, he could kill you, but that's messy, and it still wouldn't stop us from coming to look for you. No, the only answer is to buy time."

Brian took over then. "And the best way to do that is to hand you a real tearjerker. Get you out of the cabin, so he can pack up and get out of there. Or better still, send you on a wild-goose chase, all the while thinking that you're helping solve a mystery."

Trixie sank down onto the fireplace hearth. "Are you saying that I might have let the criminals get away?"

"Worse than that," Mart answered. "You might have *helped* them get away!"

Honey spoke up firmly. "You didn't see that poor man, Mart. He looked so sad and broken—not at all like the desperate, cunning criminal you make him out to be."

"That's right," said Trixie, brightening. "Everything he said made sense and fit in with all of our clues. Like that conversation I overheard. And the funny way that Eric acted the night he bought us all dinner. And what Eric said about his mother leaving that first day, and—"

"Hold it," cut in Mart. "What I want to know is where all the things that keep happening around the lodge fit in?"

"If Carl is so nice," argued Di, "then why is he trying to play ghost and scare us away?"

Trixie and Honey looked at each other and said nothing.

"You did check Carl's boot print, didn't you?" prompted Brian.

"I—I guess we were so excited about everything else that we, uh, forgot," Trixie answered.

Mart groaned in total exasperation.

Trixie didn't blame him. "It *was* kind of dumb of me not to check all the angles," she said, flopping into a chair. "Some detective I'm going to be."

"You're not such a bad detective," said Jim thoughtfully. "Look, if Carl was just handing you a line to buy getaway time, there's nothing we can do about it now, except report it to the police. But if his story is true, then we have a responsibility to keep our promise and show up at the pond tonight. And I vote for acting on the assumption that it is true."

"So do I," declared Honey.

"The only thing is," Trixie said, "we can't all go down there. That would let the kidnappers know that we're onto them."

"I don't get it," said Di.

"I can tell by the light in Trixie's eyes that she knows something we don't," Brian said to Di.

"Just this," Trixie explained. "The kidnappers have to be someone here at the lodge. They saw him talking to Eric here at the lodge, and they told Carl they'd be keeping an eye on him. Only someone staying at the lodge could do that."

"She's right!" Honey shivered. "To think we've been staying with kidnappers!"

"If all the Bob-Whites, who are supposed to be in charge of the party tonight, suddenly disappear,"

Trixie went on, "the kidnappers are going to know something is up."

"She's right again," said Mart. "Will wonders never cease?"

"So, who are our suspects?" asked Di. "Who's been acting suspicious around here?"

"Who hasn't?" Brian threw in.

"Pat and Katie do a super job running this place," began Trixie. "But we've found out that something is bothering them for sure."

"I just can't believe they could be that nasty," insisted Jim. "How about Bert and Jack? They're a tall and short pair, and they certainly are unusual."

"Jack gets to me with all his talk of ghosts," agreed Brian. "Trixie, did you ever find out what kind of boots they wore?"

"I haven't been able to check them yet," Trixie sighed.

"You know who else is suspicious?" asked Mart. "That honeymoon couple. He's tall, and she could pass for a short guy. They stick to themselves almost all the time. Hardly anyone ever sees them."

"You're not supposed to see a lot of honeymooners, silly," Di giggled.

"Who's to know if they're really honeymooners?" asked Jim.

"It can't be them," answered Trixie. "I think it's got to be either Jack and Bert or Pat and Katie."

"But there're all kinds of tall people connected with short people," Mart objected. "What about Mrs. Fleming? She's tall, and Linda and Wanda are both short.

They could keep an eye on Eric, and they could use the money to help pay Jenny's doctor bills."

Trixie squirmed. "But Carl said the tall kidnapper was a man. Besides, they could never spend a bunch of counterfeit money in a small town. It's already been spotted, and it's only been passed once."

"Okay," said Mart. "But there are other people here at the lodge, people from out of town."

"I still don't think it could be anyone but Bert and Jack or Pat and Katie," Trixie maintained.

Even Honey was baffled by Trixie's stubbornness. "I can see that both couples could keep an eye on Eric and that they could spend the money elsewhere, especially Bert and Jack. Or the O'Briens, when they move. But why can't it be anyone else?"

"Because whoever is forcing Carl to do the counterfeiting wanted to make sure that the money was good," explained Trixie. "And you can bet that they were there to see Eric pass the money."

Jim whistled. "And Pat and Katie and Bert and Jack were all at the Purple Turnip that night."

"Along with a bunch of vegetables," added Mart. "Oh, this discussion is all beside the point. Carl is obviously counterfeiting on his own and is long gone by now."

"If that's the case, we'll go up to his cabin tomorrow to make sure he's gone," said Jim. "Then we'll tell the police everything we know. But tonight, at least some of us ought to be at Porcupine Pond."

"I suppose you're right," Brian said. "Jim, you and I can accompany our schoolgirl shamuses. It's a good thing Mr. Wheeler signed you up as the alternate driver. Now you can drive us in the Tan Van."

"That's too many people," Honey objected. "We're sure to be missed."

"Brian, why don't you stay and see who doesn't show up at the party?" Trixie urged. "Give us an hour or so after you find out who's missing. If we're not back then, you can come like the cavalry and rescue us."

Trixie was glad they'd had time to settle on a plan, because just then the door opened and Miss Trask walked in. It wasn't that they didn't *want* to tell her, but Trixie had given her word that no one but the Bob-Whites would know. And Miss Trask would be sure to call in the police.

Miss Trask was brimming with talk about the party. "Why don't you have an early dinner tonight?" she suggested. "Then you'll be free to help put out food and fix up a stage for the show. In fact, we could eat now."

"Oh, I almost forgot!" exclaimed Honey as they all stood up to leave. "Miss Trask knows some Robert Frost poetry. I'll bet we could sweet-talk her into reciting some of it tonight. Won't you please, Miss Trask?"

Miss Trask looked doubtful, but the others clamored so much that she could hardly say no. "Only for the Bob-Whites would I do this," she chuckled.

After dinner, Trixie noticed Eric sitting at another table and called, "Will you do something for us in the show? A song, or a ski demonstration, maybe?"

Eric shook his head. "I don't think I'll even be at the show," he called back. "Hate to miss some good moonlight skiing in fresh snow." On his way out of the restaurant, he stopped by their table and added, "I'm sure your party will be a lot of fun, though. I'll see you next year."

Once he was gone, Mart nudged Trixie. "What did I tell you? He and Carl are taking off tonight. We'll probably never see him again, period!"

Trixie ignored him and concentrated on getting out of the lodge. While Miss Trask and the others were busy with party preparations, Trixie, Honey, and Jim were hiding the Tan Van in the bushes near the Porcupine Pond turnoff. They walked a half mile down the narrow road until they came to a smaller trail that led down the steep hill to the frozen pond.

It was a heavily wooded area. After scouting around, they decided to hide on a small knoll at the top of the hill, where they could observe the entire pond. They each tucked flashlights into their parka pockets and hid their survival kits in the bushes. Once they made sure they themselves were well hidden, they began their long wait.

Their idle whisperings to each other had lasted for what seemed like an eternity, and finally Jim became restless. "It's eight-thirty, Trixie. I don't think anyone is coming. Maybe we ought to go back."

"Can't we wait just a little longer?" Trixie pleaded. "I just know that Carl was telling the truth." Trixie felt a little sick to her stomach. It was beginning to look like Mart had been right after all, and she'd actually helped the crooks escape.

Growing more miserable by the minute, she almost didn't believe it when she heard the faint rumble of a car coming down the heavily rutted road toward them. She could tell that Honey and Jim heard it, too, and she held her breath. In a few minutes, they would know who'd kidnapped Ellen Johnson.

A Meeting at Porcupine Pond • 17

TRIXIE SQUINTED as the car headlights flashed in her eyes. After the car had turned around at the end of the road, the lights dimmed and the motor fell silent. Trixie strained her eyes to see the car and felt a sharp twinge of disappointment.

"It's Pat and Katie's pickup!" she gasped.

Two figures jumped out of the vehicle and headed down the path to the pond. Both were wearing jeans and parkas, with ski masks that covered the entire face.

"I was hoping it wouldn't be Pat and Katie," Honey whispered.

"Me, too," Trixie sighed.

"Well, we've got a job to do now," Jim muttered.

As the two figures walked out onto the ice, a third figure emerged from the woods on the opposite shore. Trixie could see Carl's long white hair gleaming in the moonlight and the silhouette of a pack on his back.

Jim crept to the O'Briens' truck and carefully pulled up the hood. "Trixie," he whispered, "I need your help."

She hurried over, and he pointed to the back of the engine. "Shine your flashlight right here." He leaned way over the engine to the distributor and pulled out a wire.

"What's that?" Trixie asked.

"The coil wire. This is a little trick Tom Delanoy taught me. Here, put this in your pocket and don't lose it. That pickup can't go anywhere without it." Then, as quietly as he had opened it, Jim closed the hood.

Trixie walked over to the driver's side of the truck and swept her flashlight across the ground. In the arc of her beam was a line of footprints—waffle-stomper boot prints. She bent down to examine them. "Jim," she said tensely, "these are five-pointed stars. These prints match the ones we saw next to the tree!"

Jim sighed. "I guess that makes Pat our ghost. Even though so many clues pointed to him, I just wasn't ready for this. Boy, did I have them pegged wrong. I thought they were really great people."

"So did I," Trixie said softly.

"Come here, you two," Honey hissed. She motioned to them to join her on the edge of the knoll.

The fresh snow reflected the bright moonlight, so

they had a clear view of all that went on, even though the people on the ice were too far away for them to hear anything.

"Where's Ellen?" asked Jim. "I thought you said they were supposed to bring Ellen."

"Jeepers, I wonder why they didn't," fretted Trixie.

"You—you don't suppose they hurt her, do you?" asked Honey.

"Don't even think that," Trixie scolded, although she was already considering worse possibilities.

The three figures on the ice were pointing and waving at each other, and they were obviously angry. Eventually things calmed down, and they seemed to talk for quite a while. Trixie wished she had had the foresight to hide closer to the pond so she could have heard what was going on.

"Look," Jim whispered. "They look like they've come to an agreement of some kind. Do you suppose they could have been in this together all along?"

"No," said Trixie with a vehement shake of her head. "Otherwise Carl would never have told us about this meeting. But I sure don't understand what's going on now."

Carl was turning to leave, the pack still on his back. Pat and Katie followed him toward the edge of the pond.

"Where are they going?" worried Trixie. "We can't lose track of them now!"

Suddenly Pat raised his hand high into the air and brought it down on the back of Carl's head. Carl slumped to the ice.

"Why did he do that?" Honey gasped, tears in her eyes.

Trixie could tell that Jim was gritting his teeth. She knew what he was thinking. Her temper was about to flare up, too.

Pat bent over and propped Carl up, while Katie got Carl's backpack off. She slung it over her shoulder and headed back toward the car in front of Pat, the two of them leaving Carl lying alone on the ice.

They had taken only a few steps, when, to the Bob-Whites' horror, Pat took out his gun and brought it down on Katie's head. As she fell to the ice, Pat grabbed for the pack.

Trixie had to cup her hands over her mouth to keep from screaming.

"I just don't believe this is happening," Jim whispered fiercely.

In a matter of seconds, Pat had taken a length of rope from his pocket and tied Katie's hands behind her back. Then, swinging the pack onto his shoulders, he started running toward the pickup.

Jim, Trixie, and Honey quickly scrambled for cover. As she heard the crunch of Pat's boots coming up the hill, Trixie clenched her fists. *Capturing a man who would be so brutal to his wife and an old man was more than I bargained for tonight,* she thought.

Pat was panting heavily by the time he reached the truck. He pulled the door open and threw in the pack, shoving it over to the passenger side as he climbed in. The Bob-Whites heard a whirring noise, then some muttered curses.

Trixie and Jim managed to smile faintly at each other.

The motor whirred again. After about ten seconds, the door opened. Trixie could see Pat slowly getting out of the pickup, a gun in one hand and the flashlight in the other. Aiming his flashlight at the woods, he made a full circle around the pickup before stopping. Then he put his gun in his pocket, tucked the flashlight between his knees, and started to open the hood.

"Now!" whispered Jim. He leaped out of the woods at full speed and made a flying tackle.

"What should we do?" Honey wailed as she and Trixie came out of the bushes.

"Nothing," Trixie answered. "Jim can handle him."

But as they drew closer, Trixie could see that Pat was fighting rough. Pat rolled on top of Jim, and his hand reached out for something that had fallen out of his pocket—the gun! Acting in a split second, Trixie kicked the gun just as Pat's fingers touched it. Then she snatched it up and threw it as far as she could into the woods.

When she turned back, she saw Jim surprising Pat with an uppercut to the chin. Pat, thrown off balance, fell backward and hit the ground. As if controlled by one mind, Trixie and Honey rushed to throw all their weight onto Pat's shoulders, pinning him to the ground.

"What teamwork," Jim called breathlessly as he ran to the bushes. He brought back the ropes from their survival kits. "Somehow I thought I might be needing this," he said as he tied Pat's feet together. "Hold him up so I can tie his hands behind his back," Jim instructed the two girls, who were still holding Pat.

Once Pat was securely tied up, Jim said, "I'd better go down and check on Carl and Katie."

"Jim, you stay here and rest. I'll go check on them," Honey volunteered. She disappeared down the hill.

Jim sank to the ground, exhausted, and Trixie turned to Pat, who was propped up against the truck wheel.

"You put on a pretty good act, Pat," Trixie said sorrowfully, reaching for his grotesque ski mask. "We all thought you were really nice." She yanked the mask off.

Then she gasped. "Wh-Why, you're not Pat O'Brien at all!"

Where Is Ellen? • 18

BERT MITCHELL just growled at them.

Jim's jaw dropped open. "What were you doing in Pat and Katie's truck?" he demanded.

"I'm not saying a thing to anyone," Bert snapped. "I have my rights."

"How come you didn't bring Ellen Johnson?" Trixie persisted. "I thought that was part of the deal."

"I don't know what you're talking about."

When Trixie turned to share a look of amazement with Jim, she noticed for the first time that he'd been hurt. By the light of her flashlight, she could see the blood trickling down Jim's face from a cut on his forehead, along with a badly bruised eye and puffiness around his face. Without flinching a bit, she got some bandages from her survival kit and started taking care of the cut just as she imagined Brian would.

"I didn't even feel that cut. But, boy, is my hand sore," Jim said, flexing his hand.

They heard some rustling in the bushes, and Honey appeared, followed by Carl and Jack.

Trixie turned to Bert. "It sure was nice of you to tie up Jack for us," she said sweetly.

Bert growled at her again.

"Can you believe it?" Honey panted as she came closer. "It wasn't Pat and Katie after all!"

"You dirty double-crosser!" yelled Jack.

"Shut up," snarled Bert. "Both of us are in this together."

"We must find Ellen," Carl said groggily. "They said she's okay, but they refuse to tell me where she is."

"First we have to get everyone back to the lodge," Jim decided. "And call the police. You and Jack are going to need your heads looked at by a doctor. That was no light tap Bert gave you."

"I thought I told you before that I'm a tough old coot," said Carl impatiently. "The important thing now is to find Ellen."

"As soon as I get the truck back together," Jim promised. "Trixie, give me that coil wire, will you? We can come back for the Tan Van later."

She fished in her pocket for the wire, then turned on Jack. "Why *didn't* you bring Ellen with you?"

"It was too dangerous," he explained nervously. "She's over—"

"Okay, I'll tell you the truth," Bert interrupted. "There is no Ellen. We're all in this together—Carl, Jack, and I. Carl masterminded the whole counterfeiting plan, and we were supposed to pick up the money and keep it for him. He's just trying to con you so he can make a getaway."

"That's right," said Jack. "I think you'd better stop worrying about us and concentrate on the real criminal—that old man."

Trixie hadn't missed the way Jack's mouth had fallen open when Bert had started talking. "We've met Ellen before," she said smugly. "And we're not going to play any more games. We know exactly what's been going on. We even know that you've been playing ghost," she told Bert.

"Right on the ball, aren't you?" he replied sarcastically. "When Pat first mentioned investigators coming to the lodge, I decided to put them on the trail of something far away from me. I was relieved when the investigators turned out to be a bunch of teen-agers, because then I could get you chasing ghosts."

"Except we found out you were the teen-agers that helped the police stop the gun smuggling," Jack put in angrily.

"We decided to give you a little test to find out how good you really were," said Bert, "so we pulled the lights-out routine. Figured that out in nothin' flat, didn't you? Think you're pretty smart, don't you? When you said at the Purple Turnip that you weren't on the trail of the ghost anymore, I knew you had to be taken care of."

Jim stopped working on the engine to glare at Bert. "Thus, the tree incident," he said curtly.

"I don't get your part in this, Jack," said Honey. "Are you really afraid of ghosts? Didn't you know that it was Bert playing ghost?"

"I played my part pretty well," Jack boasted. "My job was to talk about ghosts at all the right times. If you had followed the clues you were supposed to, you'd be chasing a ghost now instead of giving us a headache."

Finally Jim got the engine purring, and after tying Bert and Jack securely in the back of the truck, the others squeezed into the cab.

"Tell us what happened down there," Trixie said to Carl once Jim had the truck moving. "We could see what was going on, but we were too far away to hear a thing."

"They told me that they couldn't bring Ellen with them," Carl sputtered. "They said it was too dangerous, so they would just tell me where she was. I wasn't about to go for a deal like that. If those thugs hurt Ellen, I'll—"

"Did they give you any clues as to where she might be?" Honey asked quickly.

"They said there was too much danger of an avalanche where she is. They were afraid after they almost got caught in one after the big snowstorm we had last Saturday."

"That's the snowstorm we arrived in," Trixie told Carl. "That's when I saw you in the woods. I guess you were looking for your daughter."

Close to the lodge, they saw Bert and Jack's little rented car in a ditch off the road.

"Their own car couldn't make it through all the new snow," jeered Trixie, "so they stole Pat and Katie's four-wheel-drive truck."

"And fooled us," added Honey.

Jim pulled into the parking lot and let Honey out. "Honey, why don't you get Pat and Katie and Miss Trask and the others back to our suite? Trixie and I can get Bert and Jack in the back way. That way we won't disturb the party."

All the others were at the suite by the time Jim, Trixie, and Carl came in with Bert and Jack.

"We were so worried!" said Di, throwing her arms around Trixie. "As soon as Mart introduced Bert and Jack and they didn't appear, we knew what was going on."

"We were going to give you ten minutes more," added Brian.

Katie left to fetch a doctor, then Jim called the police. "They're coming right over," he announced, turning to Bert and Jack. "I guess you'll be beginning the new year behind bars."

"Are you three all right?" Miss Trask asked. "I could tell you've been working on some kind of case, but this is more than I expected."

"Will someone *please* tell me what's going on?" begged Pat.

"What about the party?" Trixie asked. "Mart, shouldn't you and Di be out there telling everyone what to do?"

"And miss another thrilling, death-defying installment in the life of Trixie Belden? Are you kidding? We asked Linda and Wanda to take over the show for us."

"I'm glad to see you're getting my name straight," Trixie joked weakly. Then she sat down on the fireplace hearth and briefly filled Pat and Miss Trask in on the tale. When she was through, Miss Trask sighed and Pat wiped his forehead.

"All that under my very nose, and I didn't even see it," Pat commented incredulously.

Carl stood up impatiently. "We've got to find Ellen. They said she's near an avalanche area. She may be . . . h-hurt."

Pat looked concerned. "Unfortunately, there're all kinds of places right now where there's avalanche danger."

"Maybe we can find a map in their room," Honey suggested.

Katie returned with the doctor, and while he examined Jim, Carl, and Jack, the girls accompanied Pat to search Bert and Jack's room. They found it totally stripped of Jack's and Bert's belongings.

"How about that!" exlaimed Pat. "They were going to leave without paying their bill."

"See if you can find any clues," Trixie urged. "Honey and I'll check their car."

The two girls walked out into the snowy parking lot and down the hill toward Bert and Jack's car. They still had their flashlights with them, and Trixie was able to see luggage in the backseat. "I guess they were going to come back for it after they got the money," she said.

She opened the car door and checked the glove compartment. "Gleeps, look at this! A one-way plane ticket from Groverville to Boston for tonight's flight. So Bert was planning to double-cross Jack all along. There's only one ticket!"

Honey shuddered. "I sure would hate to have Bert as a friend."

"I'm just so worried about Ellen out in those woods," said Trixie. "They probably haven't taken her food for quite a while if she's someplace where there's avalanche danger. And it's been snowing so long. She could die of exposure!"

"Don't talk that way," Honey said. "Besides, I don't think even Bert and Jack would leave her out in the open. She must be in a tent or some kind of natural protection."

Trixie motioned for Honey to be quiet. Off in the bushes, they heard a rustling sound. Someone was coming through the woods toward them. Trixie, her heart thumping, froze in fear. Had Jack and Bert escaped? Was there another member of the gang they didn't know about?

As the rustling grew louder, Trixie and Honey crouched behind the car, hoping against hope that they wouldn't be seen.

Then Trixie peeked over the edge of the car and saw who it was.

"Eric!" Trixie called as she jumped out from behind the car.

Eric almost fell off his skis. "Don't do that to people," he gasped. "You nearly gave me a heart attack."

Trixie wasn't listening. "The kidnappers have been caught!" she yelled. "And we know where your mother is!"

A Very Happy New Year • 19

WHAT?" Eric and Honey cried in the same voice.

"We don't have any idea where she is," Honey protested.

"Is she all right?" demanded Eric.

"We don't know, Eric," Trixie admitted. "The kidnappers didn't have her with them. But they gave us enough clues to figure out where she is."

"Trixie Belden, what are you talking about?" cried Honey.

"They said she was near where an avalanche was," Trixie told her. "It's what you just said that brought everything together."

"What did I say?"

"That she has to be in some protected area. Remember when Mart got caught in that avalanche? We had just seen a masked skier on the other side of the snowfield. And remember Di telling us about seeing caves on the hill across the river? Ellen must be in one of those caves, and that must have been Jack who we saw, probably taking her food!"

"Trixie, you're right!" Honey squealed.

"What are we waiting for? Let's go!" said Eric.

When Trixie, Honey, and Eric stormed into the suite with their news, everyone clamored to go with them. Only Katie and Miss Trask elected to go back to what was left of the party. The doctor wouldn't allow Carl or Jim to leave the suite. The pair were furious until Brian pointed out that the police, who were expected any minute, would need their testimonies before arresting Bert and Jack. Besides, someone had to stay behind to guard the kidnappers.

Pat located a rescue litter to carry Ellen back to the lodge, in case it was necessary. He also found lantern helmets to help them see better in the woods.

After what seemed like days of skiing, they came to the field where Mart had been caught. There was evidence that some smaller slides had occurred, so Pat insisted that the group cross the field in pairs, with each pair waiting until the couple ahead was safely on the other side before starting across. Pat was the last to cross.

As carefully as possible, they skied along the edge of the woods and down the steep length of the snowfield. At the bottom of the hill, they stopped to catch their breath. The frozen river lay below them, twisting its way through the canyon. Di pointed around the bend to where the caves should be, but it was too dark to see them.

"I remember those caves," said Pat. "You can see them from a side road off the main highway. That must be how Bert and Jack found them."

"How do we get across the river?" worried Trixie.

"There's an old suspension bridge not too far from here," said Pat. "After we get across, we'll have to ski along the edge of the canyon for a while, because it banks almost into the cliff. Then we'll have to climb up the rock face of the cliff to get to the caves. It really isn't very steep, but with the new snow it may be slippery. This is not going to be an easy rescue," he sighed.

Trixie was silent. She just hoped that someone would be there to be rescued.

Pat led them to the suspension bridge, which looked like a ribbon of snow dangling in the air, with a rope railing on either side. Slowly, in single file, the group set out to cross the dangerously swaying bridge. Trixie hung her ski poles around her wrists and held on to the rope railings tightly, making sure she never let go with both hands at the same time.

The pathway along the canyon's rim was even scarier. On one side was a wall of rock, on the other a twenty-foot drop onto frozen ice. Finally the path began to widen, and Pat called out, "Look ahead." In the beam of his helmet light were two caves.

After dropping the litter and taking off their skis, they all cautiously made their way up the rocky cliff to the first cave. Nothing but cold, damp darkness was there to greet them.

"She'd better be in the other cave," said Eric grimly.

"Don't even think that she might not be," said Pat. "I have a feeling that Trixie's never wrong."

Trixie gulped. She knew she was wrong lots of times. She had been wrong about Eric and about Pat himself. Maybe she shouldn't have sounded so confident when she said she knew where Ellen was.

Eric hurried to lead the way to the second cave. As he entered it, he yelled, "Mother!"

A muffled scream answered him.

By the time Trixie reached the happy twosome, Ellen Johnson was sitting up against the side of the cave, and Eric had removed her gag and was working at the ropes around her wrists and ankles. By the light of the lantern helmets, Trixie saw a couple of paperback novels and the charred remains of a fire. It did not look like a nice place to spend two weeks.

"How—how is Dad?" Ellen managed to ask. "He didn't make the money for those crooks, did he?"

"He's okay," Eric said soothingly. "He made the money, but the crooks have been caught."

"I'm so glad," sighed Ellen.

The others gathered around Eric and Ellen, saying nothing, but grinning widely. Finally Pat said, "Honestly, Eric, the least you could do is introduce your mother."

"Just a minute," Eric mumbled, still working on the ropes around Ellen's wrists.

"They're very expertly tied," said Ellen. "I tried

constantly, but I wasn't able to loosen these ropes."

"Your kidnappers were merchant marines," Trixie explained. "Sailors are very good at tying knots." Then she was silent. Maybe no one cared about Bert and Jack, now that Ellen was safe.

"How are you? Did they hurt you?" Eric demanded.

"I think I'm basically okay," Ellen replied. "I'm just so glad to see you. I heard voices coming up the cliff, but I thought it was the kidnappers. I wasn't about to get excited for them."

Eventually Eric untangled the ropes and made the introductions. Ellen smiled at each of them. It was obvious that Eric had inherited his perfect white teeth and easy manner from her.

"I can't thank you enough," she said. When she tried to stand up, her wobbly legs wouldn't hold her, and she collapsed into Eric's arms. "All I need is a little practice," she said weakly. "It's been a while."

"Oh!" Honey cried. "I was so happy to see you I'm forgetting myself. Katie sent some sandwiches and hot soup for you."

"How thoughtful of her, whoever she is," said Ellen. "One of the kidnappers—the short one, I believe—brought me sandwiches and fruit every day. But he didn't come today, and I'd give anything for something warm to drink. The one bright spot in this whole thing is discovering that so many people I don't even know care about me."

After Ellen had taken some nourishment, Eric and Brian supported her back down the cliff to where Pat was arranging blankets in the litter. They helped her into it and secured the blankets around her. Then the whole group carefully made their way back down the narrow path and to the lodge.

Ellen protested vigorously against going to the hospital. The kidnappers had been taken into custody by the police, and she wanted to spend some time resting with Carl and Eric and her new friends. Mart and Jim built a toasty fire in the fireplace, while Carl and Eric helped Ellen onto the couch and the doctor began his check. Katie hurried to the lodge kitchen to bring back enough food for everyone, and Miss Trask made tea in the suite's kitchen. Pat and Brian went to check on the party and tell Linda and Wanda to join the crowd in the Bob-Whites' suite. Di and Honey ran to get pillows and blankets for Ellen, and Trixie just sat on the couch, so happy she couldn't think of anything to do or say.

After everyone was settled around the fireplace, Trixie and the others told the whole story from the beginning.

"I just can't believe how you figured this whole thing out, Trixie," Pat said when she was through. "Did you always know it was Bert and Jack, or did you ever think it might be someone else?"

Trixie turned beet red. "Well, there were a couple of other suspects at one time, but that doesn't matter now."

"Why, Pat!" cried Katie. "I think by the way Trixie's blushing that *we* must have been her other suspects. Is that true, Trixie?"

"We did jump to a few wrong conclusions," Trixie

admitted in a sheepish voice.

Mart nodded energetically.

"What could have possibly made you think it was us?" asked Pat.

"Well, you talked about how you were being forced to leave the lodge," Trixie said hesitantly. "And you said you wished you had enough money to buy a place in the country. You had opportunity to do all the strange things that the ghost was supposed to have done. And you were there the night that Eric passed the phony money at the restaurant."

"Heavens, it does sound as if we are guilty!" exclaimed Katie.

"Didn't you know what I was talking about when I said that we had to leave the lodge?" asked Pat.

The Bob-Whites shook their heads.

"I never would have mentioned it if I'd known that," said Pat apologetically. "My contract as caretaker for the lodge is with the corporation that owns it now," he explained. "That contract terminates as soon as someone else buys the lodge, putting me out of work and out of a home."

"I'm sure that Daddy will want to keep you on," Honey insisted.

"No, one of the consultants for your father has already told me that professional lodge directors will be brought in to run the lodge. Your father's plans really put me in a bind. As much as I'd love to keep this job, I still want to see Mead's Mountain turned into a natural recreation area."

Trixie jumped up. "Jeepers! You and Katie are what

make this lodge so special. It's not like going to a big professionally run ski resort. It's like—like visiting someone else's home for a few days!"

"You've got to stay," Di wailed. "You and Katie are number one on my like list."

The other Bob-Whites all agreed enthusiastically that the O'Briens' creation of a homey atmosphere was a tremendous part of the lodge's appeal.

Miss Trask spoke up. "Don't forget that Mr. Wheeler and Mr. Kimball are going to take your report into careful consideration, although heaven knows what they're going to make of all your adventures here! Perhaps you could recommend that Pat and Katie be made the lodge directors, with some assistants to help them."

"Fantastic idea!" whooped Trixie. "This lodge is going to need lots of people. Maybe even some architectural help," she added, throwing a sly glance at Eric.

"And people like Linda and Wanda," Honey put in. "Why, the lodge would be a perfect place to sell Jenny's puzzles!"

By this time, everyone in the room was beaming at the Bob-Whites, and Pat was leaping up to hug Katie.

"You're going to recommend that Mr. Wheeler buy the lodge *and* keep us on as managers?" asked Pat incredulously.

"This is too good to be true!" Katie exclaimed.

"What a week this has been," said Mart lightly. "Ghosts, Trixie Belden, counterfeiting, Trixie Belden, kidnapping, Trixie Belden. . . ."

"Don't forget the avalanche, 'twin,'" teased Trixie, giving him a poke.

"Trixie Belden and the Bob-Whites have been solving everyone's problems today," Carl mused. "I've decided to make you a special, one-of-a-kind print of a Bob-White as my special thanks."

The Bob-Whites all gasped with pleasure.

"Wow!" Di breathed. "Our very own Carl Stevenson print!"

"Gleeps, you're terrific, sir!" cheered Trixie. "We'll give it a place of honor in our clubhouse!"

Suddenly the door to the suite flew open, and Rosie burst into the room.

"Rosie," Katie scolded. "We've taught you better manners than that. Now, go back outside and knock."

"But, Mama, it's almost midnight. Listen!"

Sure enough, the people in the lobby were counting down the seconds till midnight. "Five . . . four . . . three . . . two . . . one . . ."

In one voice, the Bob-Whites and their friends shouted, "Happy New Year!" and then they all were hugging each other. As Pat and Katie left to get champagne for everyone to toast in the new year, Trixie slipped into her bedroom and out onto the balcony.

Above the dark woods was the peak of Mead's Mountain, gleaming in the moonlight. *What a wonderful place to finish off a great year,* she thought. *I wonder what new places and mysteries this year will bring. If it's anything like last year, what a very happy new year it will be, indeed!*

22
IN A SERIES
TRIXIE BELDEN
and the
MYSTERY AT
MEAD'S MOUNTAIN